Where is Ana Amara?

An International Thriller

by

G. C. Eick

Blue Cedar Press
Wichita, Kansas

Title: *Where is Ana Amara?*
Author: G. C. Eick
Copyright © G. C. Eick, 2024

Previous edition, *The Hard Verge: Britain 2025*
Copyright © Gretchen Eick 2019

Editor: Laura Tillem
Front Cover photo: Sallye Wilkinson
Back Cover photo: Gretchen Eick
Cover design: G. C. Eick
Interior: Gina Liaso, Integrita Productions, Inc.

ISBN: 978-1-958728-18-5 (paperback)
ISBN: 978-1-958728-19-2 (ebook)

Library of Congress Control Number: 2024930300

This book is a work of fiction based on considerable research. See Notes. The characters bear no resemblance to actual people living or dead and historical figures referred to are used fictionally. All rights reserved. No part of this book may be reproduced electronically or otherwise except for brief quotes in reviews or articles without the express written permission from the author.

Table of Contents

Prologue 1
Chapter 1 5
Chapter 2 13
Chapter 3 17
Chapter 4 19
Chapter 5 25
Chapter 6 29
Chapter 7 33
Chapter 8 35
Chapter 9 41
Chapter 10 43
Chapter 11 49
Chapter 12 51
Chapter 13 57
Chapter 14 63
Chapter 15 67
Chapter 16 69
Chapter 17 73
Chapter 18 75
Chapter 19 77
Chapter 20 79
Chapter 21 83
Chapter 22 89
Chapter 23 93
Chapter 24 97
Chapter 25 101
Chapter 26 107
Chapter 27 109
Chapter 28 115
Chapter 29 119
Chapter 30 121
Chapter 31 123
Chapter 32 125

Chapter 33	131
Chapter 34	133
Chapter 35	137
Chapter 36	139
Chapter 37	143
Chapter 38	145
Chapter 39	147
Chapter 40	151
Chapter 41	153
Chapter 42	155
Chapter 43	157
Chapter 44	159
Chapter 45	165
Chapter 46	169
Chapter 47	171
Chapter 48	175
Chapter 49	177
Chapter 50	179
Chapter 51	185
Chapter 52	187
Chapter 53	189
Chapter 54	191
Chapter 55	193
Chapter 56	197
Chapter 57	201
Chapter 58	205
Chapter 59	207
Chapter 60	211
Epilogue	215
Notes	217
About the Author	219

ACKNOWLEDGMENTS

With deep appreciation to Laura Tillem, Michael Poage, Jan Farndale, and the many others who strengthened this book with their feedback and editorial advice. Also to the Blue Cedar Press Board for believing in the importance of my novels.

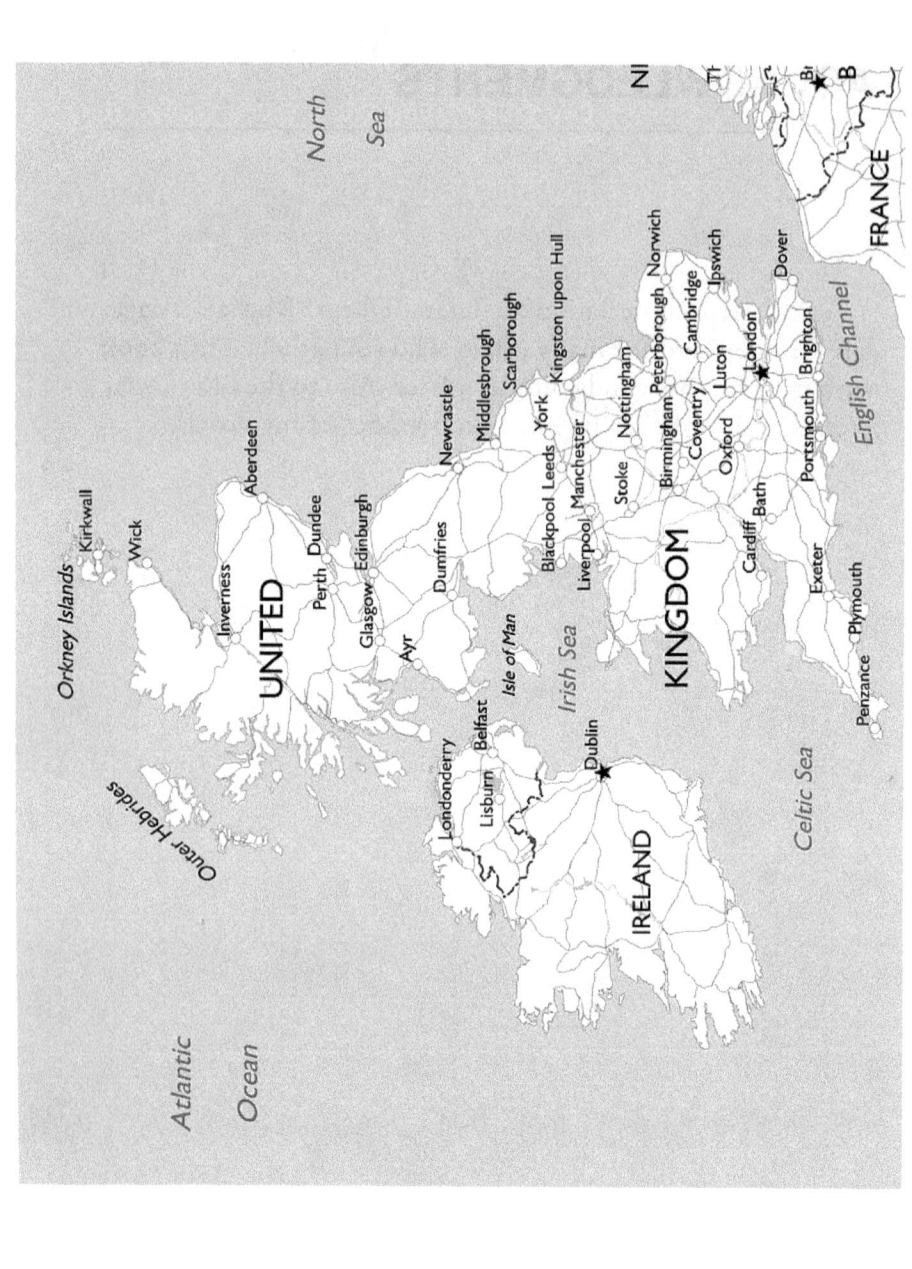

PROLOGUE

I lost myself in unexpected grief the night I met Jennifer. We both had enrolled in a community education course on the History of the Middle East. The professor was a young Brit with a closely trimmed beard and intense eyes peering through his dark framed glasses. He knew a lot about his subject. That night he lectured on Syria. I did not notice the young British woman sitting beside me. My attention was focused on the speaker. I wanted to learn what this foreign expert knew about my country.

I didn't wear the hijab at that time. I was trying to blend into my adopted country, grateful for refuge. I was all right until the screen filled with images of Homs, streets obliterated, people scattered like rag dolls among the rubble, startling puddles of crimson against the gray haze of smoke that hung in the air where the bombs had landed.

The photographs triggered images preserved forever on my retina. I did not know where I was or what was real. I began to tremble. I could barely restrain a howl birthed in my cavern of horror. I must disguise my panic. I pulled myself to standing and, choking my urge to run, forced myself to walk out of the classroom.

I was unaware that the woman seated beside me had followed me. In the women's toilet I sat in the farthest stall, huddled into myself and breathing rapidly, unable to stop the images scrolling behind my eyelids. After many minutes, I heard a female voice speaking softly. "Do you want to talk about it? It's okay either way." I remained silent for a long time, trying to breathe normally, stifling the gasps that like tics took over my body. I assumed the stranger had left.

When I recovered enough to leave the stall, I saw her leaning against the window sill. She wasn't even checking her phone. She didn't speak, just waited. I moved to the sink and splashed my face with water, avoiding her. "No one should go through such a scary place alone. Want to go for a coffee?" she said.

I didn't want to go, yet I found myself, silent and robotic, shuffling after her. In the next hour while we sat in the darkest corner of the cafeteria, I cried the tears I had suppressed for a decade. She followed me into my Pit and listened closely to my story. She helped me bear my memories.

Later she encouraged me to reach for other memories that I thought the war had obliterated, memories of when we laughed and joked, ate special foods for Bairam, sang traditional songs, and walked the countryside picking pomegranates and figs. After several months I moved into her home with my younger brothers and for the last three years flourished under her care.

When my night terrors came and I heard again the whoosh of the bombs and the frantic cries of parents seeking their little ones under the rubble, Jennifer would turn on a light, wake me up and listen, one hand resting softly on mine. When my flood of words subsided, she would hold me. Then she would fetch me a glass of pomegranate juice. I've never known where she found pomegranate juice.

Once I told her I did not want her to stay with me out of pity. "I am like a blind and lame cat that stumbled into your space and you had to take me in." Her eyes ran like fountains at my words.

"Can't you see how deeply I love you, Ana?" she said. "You are the most interesting, intelligent, beautiful person I have ever known. What you have gone through has strengthened and deepened you. I am so lucky to know you, to love you. So lucky."

One day she found a street market that sold fresh figs and bought all the shopkeeper had. That night the four of us devoured them, our mouths dripping with their sweetness. We were giddy, gorging on the happy memories carried in the taste of those figs. Even my brother Mohammed was laughing.

Jennifer jokes that I rescued her from a bland British life, that I turned her from a scientist who dabbled in social work to an advocate for the rights of those the Ultra Party terms "enemies of Britain." She supports the work I do with refugees and asylum seekers, and she will support it even now, I know. Even if it means we may never be together again.

CHAPTER 1

She was late leaving work, late catching the Tube, and rain spilled from the sky into the streets. Not a steady London drizzle, this. More like an avalanche of water surging at you from all sides. She could feel her feet sloshing in her shoes. The light over the door was out and she couldn't find the damn key. She stood on the step balancing the umbrella and a bag of dampening bread she'd bought at the corner market, while one wet hand felt in her bag felt for the house key. Her fogged glasses complicated inserting the key but, finally, she turned it, pushed against the swollen door and stumbled over the threshold.

The smell of something burning assaulted her nostrils and seized up her throat. The kitchen was straight ahead, barely visible through the gray haze that drifted toward the open door. Black smoke rose from a pot on the stove wafting up and out into the hallway. Coughing, she moved quickly into the kitchen and felt for the knob that would turn off the burner. It was scorching hot and her hand jumped from it. Using the front of her jacket as a potholder she grabbed the handle and lifted the offending pot, swiveling her body to move it into the sink. Smoke burned down into her lungs and her eyes watered so that she could barely locate the sink. As the heat penetrated through her jacket to her hand, the pain from her seared palm registered in her brain, and she dropped the pan. With a giant crack like a gunshot the bottom of the pot separated from its body as it hit the sink. She reached for the tap and turned on the cold water. Billows of steam surged upward through the dark smoke as she pushed her throbbing hand under the tap for several minutes. Then, wrapping a dish towel around her hand, she staggered toward the doorway to the dining room. The dining room, too, was clotted with smoke. She croaked, "Ana!" but the final syllable stuck as it tried to leave her throat. There was no answer.

She moved toward the desk next to the front door where they kept the landline. She was surprised to find it resting on the desk with its green engaged light blinking and a mechanical female voice repeating, "Please hang up and try your call again." She wondered how long the voice had been making that request.

Panic cramped her stomach. Where was Ana?

She pulled herself up the stairs, holding gingerly onto the bannister with her turbaned burned hand, her other hand pushing against the wall for support. It was even smokier upstairs. The smell hung on the draperies and bedclothes, ominous and insistent.

Their room looked as she had left it, bed made with Ana's usual precision, clothes picked up from the chair where she had tossed them when she'd hurried off to work knowing she was late. The belt to her fleece robe trailed from under the closet door crimson and wiggly like a stream of blood. It was unlike Ana not to tuck it away. Ana would have taken time to arrange it properly over the hook in the closet, clucking to herself that she shouldn't have to pick up other people's droppings.

The other two bedrooms were equally pristine except for the smoke hanging like a shroud over the beds. But the red belt snaking from under the closet door and the burning pot left no doubt that something was wrong.

She checked the bathroom feeling a familiar rush of terror left over from her childhood. When she was a kid and the first one home to an empty house, she had felt that terror daily as she checked each room while saving the most frightening of all, the bathroom, for last. Now as then she marshalled her courage, pushed open the bathroom door and, with fear rising like bile, threw back the shower curtain. Now, as then, no monster lurked in wait for her.

Where was Ana?

The silence overpowered her and she sank onto the toilet seat. She closed the bathroom door and opened the window to let out the smoke. The pain in her palm demanded attention. She filled the sink with cold water, unwrapped her hand and rested her arm on the edge of the sink, hand dangling down into the water. Relief reached her brain and for a moment she forgot her fear. With her left hand she opened the medicine cabinet, her hand remembering the tube of zinc oxide and the box of gauze pads on the second shelf. The zinc oxide fell heavily into the sink splashing water onto her trousers. When she reached for it, she felt the packet of 4 x 4 gauze pads in their waxed paper sleeve settle softly on the back of her hand, then float as listless as something dead on top of the water.

She tore open the gauze and, using her teeth, unscrewed the cap on the zinc oxide. She dried her pulsing palm with the hand towel that hung next to the sink. She applied the dressing. Better. She stood to look for tape, found it, and wrapped it around her painful palm, constructing a rather sloppy bandage. She opened the windows in the bedrooms and flipped the switch that turned on the attic fan that made a great clattering noise as though a regiment of armed men were rushing the enemy.

She returned to their room as the smoke dissipated, looking for signs of Ana's having been there. Nothing appeared out of place. Nothing was missing. Except Ana.

She descended the stairs and removed her keys from the front door. She locked the inner door and kept the wooden door open to air the house. That's when she noticed Ana's handbag sitting upright on the chair beside the front door, where she always positioned it so she wouldn't have to hunt for it when something came up that required her to leave this sanctuary in a hurry. Jennifer found it hard to swallow. Ana's handbag, intact! Wallet, money, credit cards, lip gloss, breath mints, a packet of tissues— only her mobile phone was missing.

The mail pooled just inside the threshold bore a smeared shoeprint. Jennifer must have walked right over the mail as she charged into the house. She scanned it now as though it might tell her where this woman, her dearest companion and the love of her life, might have gone. Only ads from the local COOP and a catalog featuring women in fashionable headscarves looked back at her. Nothing more.

They had met in grad school three years ago in a class on the history of the Middle East. Ana had come from Syria in 2014 and was living with her two younger brothers in a tiny apartment in a complex that catered to internationals. In those days she wore trousers and loose shirts that covered her arms and legs, but no head scarf. Her dress was a kind of compromise between her inclination to declare herself as Muslim while not offending the Islamophobic people with whom her life intersected every day. Her brothers, on the other hand, with their casual drinking, jeans and T-shirts, appeared entirely Westernized. They dated British girls whose uncovered arms and legs and half visible breasts cradled in push-up bras left Ana feeling embarrassed for them, she had told Jennifer.

As months passed, Ana had responded to growing anti-Muslim sentiment in Britain with nonverbal defiance. When the local media complained about women they called "jihadists" being a danger to the country—"who knows what they may be hiding beneath their loose clothing!"—when they warned the public that women wearing burqas or face coverings might well be terrorists and editorialized that they should be body searched at the airport and subway, Ana began to cover her hair with a headscarf. She said she wanted to show solidarity. "We came here because of freedom of expression. Stereotyping Muslim women who exercise that freedom by covering their hair is blatant hypocrisy." She said that at dinner the night she first began to wear hijab.

That was a year ago. Shortly after that, they'd moved in together, Ana and her brothers sharing this house that Jennifer had bought after a major promotion made it possible to manage a mortgage. Some months later Jennifer and Ana began sharing the bedroom with the king-sized bed. This triggered Ana's older brother Mohammed who, outraged and dismissive, erupted that evening and called his sister the worst names he could think of because she shared a bed with a woman. The next day both brothers moved out. There had been no contact with them since.

Jennifer hated to see Ana's family split, hated being the cause. Being a transplanted Muslim in Britain was hard enough without losing what was left of your family. This family had fled the horrors of war and lost both parents as well. It was common knowledge that since the Ultra Right won the election two years ago the UK government was tapping their phones, tracking their movements, monitoring their email. Not only Muslim women wearing burqas or headscarves, or those with Muslim names, were on the watch list now. Sympathetic Brits, taunted as "wannabe ragheads," were also under surveillance, according to reports in *The Guardian*. Rumor had it that even changing your name wouldn't protect you. Those who were open about their religion were under special government scrutiny.

Ana was a freelance journalist working with Human Rights Watch and Amnesty on the plight of Muslim asylum seekers. Once her brothers moved out, she had begun using the bedroom her brothers had vacated as her office. She said she felt safer working from home. She could research and write her articles for online media covering the war in Syria and, when she needed to interview people, meet them after dark. Anonymity was important and darkness supplied the illusion of anonymity. Could it be that Ana had rushed off to help another asylum seeker taken into custody by the police? But it was totally unlike her to leave without taping a sticky note to the refrigerator that said where she was and when she'd be back. She would never leave with a pot cooking on the stove, the landline off the hook, and her handbag sitting by the front door.

Jennifer hurried downstairs to check the shiny surface of the fridge in case she'd missed a note. Spotless and empty. It reflected only her worried face. Ana was intolerant of clutter. She said when you are a refugee, you learn to minimize. You never know when you will have to move at a moment's notice.

Surely she wouldn't move without telling me?

Jennifer wondered if she should call her parents. She and Ana assumed her parents' phones, too, were tapped. Her parents were good people, optimistic and progressive, part of Britain's dwindling middle class here in the capital city. She needed their optimism, their confidence in the government, a confidence she was raised with. She needed their common sense and their reassurance that everything would be all right.

"Mum." She tried to keep her voice even. She and Ana had made a game of it, this effort to make those listening in work for anything they got. "Could you drop by tonight?"

She heard her mother's reluctant sigh. Mum was so transparent. Probably she was already in her pajamas nestled beside Dad watching the evening news.

"I have to get dressed, but I'll be there in twenty-five minutes, love," Mum replied. Jennifer could count on Mum to come through for her.

The smoke had mostly dissipated with the ceiling fans and open doors and windows. Jennifer placed the remains of the fractured pan in the trash and heated water for a pot of cinnamon tea, Mum's favorite. Realizing that it had been nine hours since she'd eaten, she nosed about in the fridge and located a jar of Ana's homemade yogurt, some pita, and Ana's hummus that tasted of cumin and garlic. By the time Mum arrived, she was sated and her problem-solving mode had kicked in.

They sat together at the kitchen table with the radio playing slow jazz to obscure their voices and entertain those listening in.

"Love, she must have been called away to an interview she couldn't pass up. I'm sure she'll be home soon." Although she needed Mum's reassurance, Jennifer knew better. "Could she have gone to see her brothers? Maybe she got word that they were in some kind of trouble and just flew out the door to help them. You know that's how she'd respond. She's missed them so much....Maybe I should stay the night with you. Would that help?"

She so loved her Mum's eagerness to be helpful, but Mum's optimism wasn't helping tonight and eventually Mum went home to her own house.

It was one a.m. when Jennifer went to bed, leaving the porch and hall lights on for Ana, just in case. The streetlights shone through the bedroom window glaring and intense as an interrogation lamp. She'd forgotten to draw the curtains, or maybe she'd been afraid to. Her fear pulled her to Ana's side of the bed and she nuzzled Ana's pillow seeking the slight scent of jasmine Ana's graceful neck had left behind. It was a long night.

She woke to the sun ambling hopefully across the quilt and alighting on her face.

CHAPTER 2

Professor Ibrahim emerged from the office of the Chair of his department frowning. He didn't know what to do with his anger. He had published in four professional journals this year and had written half a dozen grant proposals, although they'd all been declined. He knew he was the most productive of the junior faculty. So how could his department chair rationalize not granting him tenure? He'd thought the man had more spine. Probably he'd over estimated him.

He had no class after this and no office hours either, so he loaded up his briefcase and left, stopping for a cup of strong coffee in the student union before deciding he needed to process his anger with someone. He called his only friend in chemical engineering and asked if they could talk. Ahmed Zafar was from Pakistan and might add some perspective to Ibrahim's speculation.

Ahmed suggested they meet half way. It was a nice enough day and they could talk sitting on the bench beside the Rodin statue of clasped hands.

Ahmed listened to him without interrupting, his legs outstretched, and his eyes fixed on his shoes until Ibrahim finished. Ahmed was fifteen years older than Ibrahim, his shiny black hair streaked with gray. Ahmed was tenured. He spoke carefully, taking time with each word.

"I've been worried about this. The climate is not good for us now. Everyone is suspicious of us, no matter how long we've lived here or how obvious we are about our British patriotism. It's like quicksand, sucking us down. What you're saying doesn't surprise me, but it makes me sad. I've raised my three children here, my wife's a doctor, I'm a published scholar—but…sometimes I wonder if I made a mistake remaining here once I earned my PhD. The past twenty-five years it's gotten steadily worse for us and there seems to be nothing we can do about it."

Ahmed's words startled Ibrahim, who had been buried in his studies, first completing another PhD—they would not recognize his Syrian PhD—and then writing more than a dozen articles that were published in scholarly journals. There had been no time for looking beyond all the work he had to get done to qualify for tenure. It alarmed him to hear such sobering words from this man who had mentored him through the past six years teaching at this university.

"So should I challenge their decision? What do I do?"

"You could challenge it, though I don't think that will change the decision. You could go to the media. If they cover your experience, it would at least add another piece of documentation of what is happening here. But if you challenge, no other university will hire you. They don't like whistleblowers and they protect their own. You could look for a job with a community college or online university. They seem to be under less pressure, although I hear they monitor their student body pretty closely. Lots of international students, you know." Ahmed sighed audibly. His eyes scanned the pleasant tree-lined pathways that crisscrossed the campus quad. "This is a lovely campus," he said. "Why don't you come around for a meal on Saturday evening? Don't despair. This is still the UK, after all. We can talk more then." He stood and extended his hand. "I must go or I'll be late for class."

Ibrahim watched him recede toward the applied sciences building, walking fast but with measured steps as though not wanting to attract attention. He pictured the theatre classroom filled with students of all colors—the program especially attracted international students as did Ibrahim's. Ironic, he thought. They use us to teach younger versions of ourselves from whom they've received tuition far higher than they charge their own students. Then they spit them out with their newly minted degrees, incapable of returning home because six years or more away from home changes you, and your government does not want smart young people stirring things up back home. I followed their script. I did everything right, yet I am still a foreigner who will not receive the protection of tenure.

He decided not to return to the office.

He took the long route home to his apartment, walking along the riverfront for more than an hour staring blankly ahead, his legs on autopilot. As dusk descended on this dismal day, he hailed a taxi to carry him the rest of the way. The driver looked him over before unlocking the cab to let him in.

CHAPTER 3

September

Ana did not return, not the following day or week or month, and there was no word of her. Jennifer left Ana's handbag sitting on the chair next to the front door where she had found it that evening when she came home to find their house full of smoke and the smell of scorched food. It gave her comfort to see it there, as if Ana was already home. Each time she entered the house and passed the handbag she thought irrationally, surely Ana had returned. Her heart tightened its fist and flooded her body with warm anticipation and a rush of adrenalin that would momentarily cancel her anxiety. That handbag kept her going, despite the inevitable crash that followed remembering that its presence did not mean Ana was back. She would hold onto the doorway to steady herself then make her way to the couch and slide down into its overstuffed comfort where she would wait for her heart to readjust.

She managed the magnitude of her loss by studying it. She was after all a scientist and turned her powers of observation into a strategy for her own survival. She found it fascinating the sheer size of the hole in her life left by this woman's disappearance. She had known she loved Ana but the degree of her dependence on Ana's observations, her intellect, her humor, her presence stunned Jennifer. Her mind worked to untangle memories of their shared past, to analyze what it was that brought them together. She allowed herself thirty minutes each morning for this remembering. Allotting herself this time appeased that emptiness that would have kept her lying in bed all day overcome by loss.

It was important to carry on as though her life had not been severed from its moorings. Her parents checked in daily, Mum trying to be chipper but reduced to clichéd reassurance that the wobble in her voice contradicted. In the previous month most of Jennifer's friends had dropped away, usually without explanation. Recently one had the decency to tell her that National Security Investigators had been making the rounds to ask about Ana's connections with the MIP, the Movement for Islamic Purity, a group His Majesty's Government had added to its terrorist list. Later Jennifer deduced that the woman would not have explained her departure from Jennifer's life if they hadn't run into each other walking from the subway on a public street crowded with people, a setting where the surveillance cameras could probably not pick up their two minute exchange.

Looking straight ahead face taut, avoiding eye contact, her friend had whispered, "A severe faced woman, hair pulled back into a tight bun, and a stern man, both of them hard muscled and vaguely threatening, came to see me at work. They asked a lot of questions about Ana's brothers, her writing, why she rarely leaves the house, whether we knew that her father had been executed… it was pretty scary. I'm sorry but I have my own family to protect. I can't stay in contact with you."

Then she walked away, no hug, no smile. Anger at this abandonment had filled Jennifer. She had picked up her pace, desperate to see Ana's handbag on the chair by the door.

CHAPTER 4

Aaron Geronsky had made a career in the UK foreign service, starting with two years in Cuba fifteen years ago followed by two-year stints in Uzbekistan and Indonesia. It was frustrating to just get to know a place and then be transferred across the world and start over learning a new language and culture and meeting those who shaped policy for that government. In between postings he worked in the home office and enjoyed the cosmopolitan culture of the capital city. He did love his life. What better way to see the world? At least if you were assigned to a location where your family could come along. That might not be the case next time.

He was home now, living in a suburb with Marissa and their two girls and enjoying having weekends to himself. Today one small thing had disturbed his contentment. While reconciling the budget for his department in preparation for a review by Parliament, he'd found expenditures coded so that he had no idea how to count them. When he'd asked his boss, the man's expression told him he'd made a mistake.

"Refugee assistance," he had replied curtly.

Clearly it was not an expenditure for refugee assistance, which was recorded in another area of the budget. It was too much money, twice the amount identified as "Refugee Assistance." Nevertheless, he identified the mysterious entry as his boss directed. When they appeared before a parliamentary oversight committee, perhaps he would defer to his boss if there were questions about the excessive figure.

Marissa met him at the door still wearing her coat, both of them returning from work at the same time. The girls were doing homework in the dining room under Katie's supervision. He paused in the doorway to kiss Marissa and absorb the calm of home. The television was on in the kitchen. He could hear some cheerleader-peppy anchorwoman reporting the dangers of the day in a lilting voice that belied the import of her words. Supper smells and the voices of his children conferring as they worked welcomed him. The living room was half-lit by one lamp so that his eye was drawn through the door that led into the dining room where the overhead light caressed the two blond heads bent over their work. He felt Marissa behind him helping him off with his coat and turned to her smiling and grateful that this was where he belonged.

At the hearing in Westminster two days later a parliamentarian asked about the large amount of money spent for Refugee Assistance. Aaron looked at his boss who said they were having to construct new camps, there were so many coming into the country now with terrorist activity in so many parts of the globe forcing people to flee their homes and the barbaric behavior of repressive governments and guerrilla fighters who opposed them. The parliamentarian asked for a detailed report on just how this money was being used. "We need more information, I'm sure you can understand. Please notify us when you have more details and return to testify."

That was it. Except that his boss assigned Aaron the job of gathering this information and writing up the report.

"Shall I visit the camps?" Aaron had asked.

"You can write the report with or without visiting the camps. But if you want to go, go ahead." His boss said this with his back to Aaron, already busying himself with other matters.

The camps were in the underpopulated lowlands where the land was valuable primarily for its mineral resources. He decided to visit the camp in Devon west toward Bristol. He took the train from Paddington to Exeter where he booked an overnight at the Arundel Hotel and hired a car. People were surprisingly friendly, one of the benefits of country living, he guessed. Approaching his destination, he was surprised to see an eight-meter concrete perimeter wall that seemed to go for miles. It resembled the wall between Israel and the Palestinian territories he had seen on a previous posting. Barbed razor wire extended the wall upward another meter. Except for the razor wire the concrete fortress wall looked positively medieval. This was not what he had expected.

He located the driveway to the entrance and was stopped by two armed guards with giant rifles leveled at him. Flustered, he shuffled through his papers to locate the one authorizing him to visit the camp. Showing it and his passport seemed to pacify the guards, who lowered their guns and waved him through, calling out, "Have a good day, sir." It was an odd mixture, threatening weapons and cordiality.

Inside the perimeter wall dozens of one-story brick barracks extended for miles arranged along roads as straight and symmetrical as the cells on a spreadsheet. His first impression was that he had entered a wasteland, for he saw no trees and no one on the streets. Then a door in the nearest barrack opened and a smartly dressed man in a sand colored uniform approached him, right hand extended.

"Mr. Geronsky. Welcome to Camp May. I'm Officer Pendleton, assigned to take you around." They shook hands and Pendleton (he never provided his full name) guided Aaron to where he could park his car. An aide drove up in an electric car to take them on a tour the camp and they set off. Aaron had turned on his voice recognition device so he could speak his observations and capture them in print for his report.

Toward the rear of the camp men sat outside on the ground in rows facing each other's backs. They were pulverizing stones. Pendleton said this was a way to keep them busy, "good for their mental health." Aaron was reminded of a place he had visited while he served Her Majesty's Government in Botswana—South Africa's Robbin Island where Nelson Mandela and his fellow inmates had pulverized rock, at least when the International Red

Cross visited the Robbin Island Prison. Other days they quarried the rock.

"Where are the women and children?"

"The women are working in this building. They make cell phones and other small digital devices." Pendleton opened the door, nodding to the two armed guards standing inside.

Women sat at long tables under skylights and long fluorescent lamps inserting tiny parts. He was surprised to see them wearing hijabs.

Now questions poured out of him. Where did the refugees sleep? Eat? Where were the children? Were families kept together? What sort of training was provided to prepare them for work outside the camp? What countries did they come from?

Pendleton's answers were clipped. Women and children stay in separate barracks. Children learn English in the morning and in the afternoon work in the vegetable garden. They come from 150 countries. "We mix them together."

Geronsky and Pendleton said the words together: "So they must communicate in English." Pendleton flashed him the hint of a smile, then excused himself for a moment to speak with one of the "assistants." Geronsky felt a tug on his right pant leg and glanced down from his 6'3" height. All he saw was the top of a woman's covered head facing down to the small parts on the table before her. Then her arm flew out, touched his shoe and slipped something into the sliver of space between his arch and the leather.

Pendleton called him to come. Instinctively Geronsky made a choice. He would not betray the woman. Without looking at her he turned and walked to where Pendleton stood impatiently snapping his fleshy left thumb and middle finger, his doughy face wary.

"What else do you wish to see?"

"The barracks where people live?" Geronsky was puzzling where all that money for Refugee Assistance was going.

"That would violate official policy. No visitors to asylum seekers. Might endanger them."

"How do these people get here?"

"On buses and rail cars. A few by helicopter, the most important ones."

Geronsky wrinkled his forehead and tightened his lips. He was utterly confused. Refugees arriving by helicopter? Refugees from 150 nations, three-fourths of the world's countries? He was out of his depth here. He consciously slackened his face to banish signs of his confusion and concern. Taking a new tack, he extended his right hand to Pendleton, giving the officer's limp appendage a vigorous shake.

"Thank you, Officer Pendleton. This has been most helpful. If you can't show me more of the facility, I'll return to my lodgings now for a rest and return tomorrow." He surveyed the room casually, looking for the woman who had stuffed something into his shoe, but the women were uniformly dressed and as one were occupied assembling things. No one looked up.

In his hotel room Geronsky tried to recall the details of what he had seen. A warehouse filled with long tables occupied by women, most if not all of them in matching hijabs and burqas. Male "assistants" carrying semi-automatic rifles pacing between the rows of tables. No one speaking, no one smiling, each one wrapped in silence and isolation despite being in the presence of hundreds of other identically dressed women. His closest experience to this was when he went to a village in Colombia a few years ago and watched dozens of women working together weaving cloth, but those women talked and laughed as they worked. Here they were silent as armed guards policed them. It depressed and chilled him to see them, despite the afternoon sun charging through his window to deposit a large rectangle of light at his feet.

His feet! He slipped off his shoes, fingers feeling for the small folded piece of paper she had tucked into the side of his left shoe. It was more fragile than he'd imagined, not paper but tissue, single ply toilet tissue. He unfolded it to find four reddish brown letters forming a single word—HELP. The red, he realized, was blood.

CHAPTER 5

As dark moved in the guards ordered the women to stop work and tidy their work space. Each tiny part must be put into its proper plastic compartment in each woman's cubicle. Nothing could be lost, everything must be accounted for by the guard, who counted the items in each woman's cubicle and recorded them on the spread sheet on his cell phone. One missing screw could hold them up for hours sitting at attention on their unpadded benches in the factory where the preset heat went off precisely at five. They knew the routine and followed it diligently or they would miss their end of day meal, the only time they saw their children.

The pad of her middle finger traced the scab that made a ridge across her palm marking where she had pushed the screw into her skin, her finger collecting a drop of blood to make each letter. She didn't know what she hoped for, but the man with the Officer looked kind and she had to take a chance. It was growing more and more crowded in the factory and in the barracks. Food was decreasing and the guards more reckless with their weapons. Perhaps they were anxious that holding more people in the camp made their assignment to maintain Social Control increasingly difficult. Just last week the women in the warehouse had been subjected to a lecture by a pasty faced officer who told them that many more people were to join them. New camps would soon be open in the rural areas here in the middle of the country. Those who behaved well and followed orders would be the first to be removed to the newer camps with their families. His message was translated into several languages before he dismissed them.

What was causing this delay? It was nearly six and her teeth had begun to chatter. She was not alone in this. The sound of chattering teeth in the high-ceilinged room made a white noise as though hundreds of rats were chewing small stones. The overhead lights had dimmed when the guards called for them to stand and walk toward the exit, hands in front of them, palms up for inspection. Thank God for the dimmed light. When they passed through the inspection station the women alternated turning off to the right, then to the left, separated from those they worked beside for nine hours a day so that there could be no fraternization, no human interaction, no attempts to plan to resist. She made her way to her barrack, one of the ones where Muslim women were housed without their children. She had no children. She stumbled entering the barrack and fell to her knees. A tall brown-skinned woman helped her up. Was it her time of the month that made her weak? she asked. But she hadn't bled for the two months she had lived here, if she was calculating correctly. A current of worry moved through her. Could it be that she was pregnant? She had not been with a man in that way for many months, except for that horrific night when she first arrived at the camp. She had forced herself to dismiss that night, to lock it away with the other shameful things—his floggings and beatings and the cigarettes he had burned into the soft inside of her thighs and torso. Denial would prevent her from melting into despair. She had read that under great stress—for example, under slavery in the Caribbean or during the Holocaust—women frequently stopped menstruating. She held onto this fact as a mantra. The circumstances of this asylum camp must be the reason she had stopped bleeding. But the woman's question eroded her denial.

The woman helping her had a long, oval face and beautiful skin, soft and smooth and brown as newly turned earth. She was smiling kindly as she helped her up from the floor. She appeared to be from Africa. From Mali, she said, when asked. She led her to her cot and helped her lift her weary legs onto the mattress and settle herself, leaning back against the steel headboard. Then the woman went away. She returned with a bowl of thin stew in which clumps of rice rose like islands in the center of the bowl. "Thank you, Mali." She felt overwhelming gratitude for this small act of thoughtfulness and feared she might let loose her tears, which she had so far held in abeyance. "Allah will protect you, my friend," the African woman replied before turning and moving gracefully down the central corridor between the beds.

Children scurried through the barracks to find their mothers. They had learned not to call attention to themselves, not to squeal with delight or sing out when they located them. It was safest to remain invisible. She could hear mothers speaking in dozens of languages—Farsi, Urdu, Fulani, Hausa, Pashto, Dari, Uzbek, Berber, Mongolian, Kazakh, Arabic, French—calming their little ones as they led them to the huge pots from which the elderly women spooned stew and rice into the bowls of each family group. An hour must have passed this way, the sounds of babble filling the barracks with memory and hope, as mothers summoned the past to lay claim to a better future. Then the female guards ordered the children back to their barracks. They had followed this routine for months, long enough for the children to learn that if they fussed at being separated from their mothers, they would not be permitted to return for days. Women and children had learned docility. Their fear and uncertainty pushed away the hope their hour of reunion had planted. The reality of powerlessness dried up the nourishment that recalling better times with their children had provided. In lines the children marched out of the building casting looks of longing over their shoulders as their mothers slunk to their cots to endure another lonely night and the sameness of tomorrow. Without the children the barracks returned to its default silence.

CHAPTER 6

In the morning Geronsky, the agent from the foreign service, dressed quickly having processed a plan of sorts for how to handle his second day at the camp. He scrubbed his face ruddy and lathered it with shaving cream, enjoying the way his razor made a smooth path through the mound of white and then jumped from the tip of his chin like an accomplished downhill skier. He wanted to visit the children's unit, the barracks for men and those for women, and he would insist on interviewing a dozen adults before his drive to Exeter to catch the train back to London and Marissa—and sanity. It was essential that he be forceful, take command of the situation, not let Officer Pendleton keep him from his intentions.

After a lavish breakfast of fresh croissants and creamy eggs served with mushrooms and thick bacon, he drove back to the camp where Pendleton and the driver met him in the parking lot. While they rode into the camp, he laid out his plan for the day, making it clear that his requests were not optional. To his surprise Pendleton acquiesced. They entered a children's barrack. Children sat on the floor in groups of 25 learning English from young teachers who looked to be fresh out of university. Pendleton said they could not be interrupted, Aaron could not speak with them. Next they visited the men's barracks, row upon row of cots and bunk beds with toilets on both ends of each building. There was an eating area with dining tables at one end, near the exit. The men were outside at the quarry pummeling limestone into a powder that was used, Pendleton now told him, in making an impermeable substance that waterproofs wood.

Pendleton selected six men for Aaron Geronsky to speak with. They sat in a circle around him responding to his questions hesitantly and in heavily accented English. They resisted his probing, answering "no problem" repeatedly and with increasing insistence even when it was an inappropriate response to his question. He wasn't sure what was going on. Did they not understand the questions? When he asked for a translator, Pendleton said there was no one available at this time. It all seemed strange to Aaron.

"They are not to be trusted, you know," Pendleton said to him when the interview was over. "Many of them are with terrorist groups. They are jihadists who would as soon cut off your head as tell you the truth." Pendleton spit an arc of saliva into the dust with a skill Geronsky could not help admiring. "The women aren't much different. Oh, they pretend purity, covering their bodies and their heads, but you'd be shocked to know how many ask the guards to give them sexual satisfaction. A number of my men have reported this."

Geronsky was indeed shocked at Pendleton's casual assumption that these women sought sex. He knew from his postings in Uzbekistan and Indonesia that such behavior from covered Muslim women could bring a death sentence by stoning or worse. He wanted to challenge Pendleton, but he needed to collect more evidence, so he asked Pendleton to say more, confident that his voice activator was getting down everything the officer said, leaving him to indict himself.

Aaron's conversation with the women was marginally more helpful because Pendleton was called away to take a call. During his absence Aaron asked the women in Arabic how they were treated. Most lowered their eyes and remained silent, but a couple of women spoke out after glancing over their shoulders to be sure Pendleton was not within earshot. "We are separated from our husbands and children and from others from our countries. If we complain we are beaten…or worse. Why are we here? We are prisoners." Then silence. Aaron did not see Pendleton returning to their circle, but he noticed the women's faces alter, animation replaced by vacant, unfocused stares. He knew he would learn nothing else from them. He stood and thanked them all. As he left them he said, "As-Salaam Alekum," the greeting of peace he had learned from his Muslim driver on his first posting.

Pendleton said the children were now engaged in other lessons and could not be disturbed. He gave Aaron a terse smile that showed no teeth and announced that his visit to the asylum camp was over.

CHAPTER 7

Damir and Mohammed learned through the informal network of Syrian refugees that their sister had disappeared. At first they told each other it was her own fault, taking a woman as a lover. God would be displeased with her, and others in their community would be also. Perhaps her disappearance was punishment for her sin. They loved Ana but could not understand her. Why begin wearing hijab and at the same time take a woman as her lover? It was a sacrilege.

They talked about what to do for weeks. Coming up with no ideas that seemed possible, they did nothing. After a month they concluded they must talk with Jennifer, although they blamed her for leading Ana into sin and perdition. Knowing that both their apartment and Jennifer's house were probably under surveillance by security cameras, Mohammed suggested asking a non-Muslim friend to deliver a note to Jennifer. "Put it through the letter slot and then leave. Keep your head down and wear a dark hoodie like most British blokes." The young man did as he was instructed. The note simply gave a place, date and time. It was signed D & M.

Two days later, on Saturday afternoon at two, Damir and Mohammed were playing basketball in the park near their highrise apartment. It was a beautiful early-summer day, surprisingly warm, the air perfumed with the scent of roses. Mohammed noticed Jennifer coming along the footpath that circled the court. He passed the ball to his brother and excused himself for a toilet break. Instead of heading to the W.C., he followed Jennifer up the path that ran through a heavily wooded stretch that would make drone monitoring more difficult.

"Do you know what has happened to Ana?" Jennifer's voice was low and intense. She had forgotten to take time to greet them properly. Now she tried to make up for her rudeness. "Greetings. I hope you are well. Damir also? May Allah bless you both."

Mohammed's disapproval of her was clear when he too neglected the normal ritual of polite greeting and moved straight away to answer her question. "I know that others from our community have also gone missing," he told her. "Whole families as well as individuals. No word from them. Perhaps Ana was taken with these?—Or perhaps our parents' honor was defended by punishing her for her sinful behavior with you." His face reflected the wariness and hostility he felt toward this Anglo woman whom he blamed for his sister's disappearance.

"This is your country. You should know what has happened to her. We are staying out of it. We must not be deported. I know that you know something of the terror Assad has imposed on our homeland. But we know a man who used to be our professor at uni who may be able to help." Mohammed passed Jennifer a business card. Then he nodded curtly, turned and jogged back to the basketball court.

Jennifer stood as though turned to stone. She had hoped the note through her letter slot meant the past was forgiven, the brothers ready to do whatever it took to locate Ana. She was wrong.

The summer day was deceptively balmy. The forecast was for strong winds blowing in a cold front tonight. She shivered as though it had already arrived and began walking home, her right hand gripping the business card in her coat pocket.

CHAPTER 8

October

Ana had been missing for more than three months now. And Jennifer hadn't a clue what to do to find her. She turned the key and opened the front door. Ana's handbag was still there but it had tipped over. An assortment of breath mints, coins, lipsticks and pens had spilled across the entryway. Had their cat, Finn, grown bored and played with the handles of the handbag, causing its upset? Or had someone entered their house for criminal or other nefarious purposes?

Jennifer squatted and gathered up the contents of the handbag, then carried it to the dining room table, dumping everything out to see what might be missing. She had checked Ana's bag repeatedly when Ana first went missing, seeking clues that might explain her abrupt departure. She remembered everything it had contained from that first horrible day. The wallet was still there with its assortment of pound notes, credit cards, library card, membership cards for an assortment of charitable organizations. There were packaged tissues and tampons, a small mirror and a lipstick. Nothing seemed to be missing.

She noticed that the lining was torn at a seam ever so slightly. She didn't recall noticing this before. This must be Finn's handiwork. Still, she ran her forefinger through the hole and felt around in the space between the leather and the taffeta lining. Something as small as her smallest fingernail and circular like a battery stuck to the ridge where the front and back leathers were stitched together. She scraped the seam to dislodge it. After some effort she brought it out of the lining cradled in her only remaining fingernail. She'd gone back to biting her nails after Ana left, and the state of her uneven, chewed nails disgusted her.

Examination of the tiny metal disk showed it was not a watch battery or a battery of any kind. Could it be another listening device? They had scoured the house looking for them and for the cameras the TV news had reported were the latest technological devices successfully fighting terrorism. Had this disk been in the handbag all along or had it been planted by a homeland security intruder today while Jennifer was at work? Or was she being paranoid? Perhaps it was a part of Ana's cell phone or even one of her pens. Jennifer had not found the cell phone in the handbag or anywhere in the house, though she repeatedly looked for it.

Jennifer's whole body twitched as she felt terror rooting deeper and deeper in her. Sometimes she felt it in her throat, an acid taste that wouldn't go away. Sometimes her stomach betrayed her attempt to appear "normal" by afflicting her with constant, low grade nausea. At other times her bowels reminded her that her reality was anything but "normal."

She replaced the handbag, its contents restored, and pulled the business card from her coat pocket. She made herself a cup of chai and sat down again at the table studying the card Mohammed had given her. She couldn't phone the professor or text or email. Surveillance was too extensive. Perhaps she could drop by the campus posing as a returning student seeking counsel. She could go during her lunch hour. But perhaps he would not be in his office at that time. Regardless, she would go. She might leave a note using another name and her mum's phone number asking for a call back if he wasn't in. Yes, it couldn't hurt to try. And she had to do something.

She had visited the police and made a missing person report. But the officers had shown little interest, telling her that refugees seldom stay in one location. "Probably due to the trauma they have experienced, they tend to move every few months....or maybe for fear they will be picked up as illegals. Can't cope with any more of those now, can we?"

She fixed herself a simple supper and, after she had eaten, stood to do the washing up. She turned the TV to the news and was about to settle into her favorite chair in front of the television when she was diverted by the images scrolling across the screen. An anchor woman with long blonde hair and artificially whitened teeth was perkily reporting that the government had announced today it was tripling the money it would spend on refugee assistance. The divided screen showed the debate in a committee of the Commons in one panel. In the other half of the screen ran a drone video showing an aerial view of the asylum camps--rows of barracks that stretched across a broad expanse of lowlands. It showed no humans, just an immense encampment surrounded by a high concrete wall topped with rolls of razor wire. In the lower right corner of the video she read "HMDHS video." Government supplied. The camp reminded her of residential areas with newly constructed identical rectangular council flats, no trees, no variation. She'd always wondered how anyone in those places found their way to their own assigned "home." Suddenly a memory surfaced, from her secondary school trip to the continent, when her favorite teacher took them, despite the objection of some of the parents, to Auschwitz and Birkenau in Poland. Her mind's eye recalled the tedious proliferation of identical rectangular buildings--innocuous in appearance, her teacher had pointed out, but lethal. These were holding camps for populations about to be dispatched to Hitler's gas chambers, killing factories that Hitler ordered destroyed as the Allies closed in on Poland and Germany.

That was a long time ago and never to happen again, some students protested. They were parroting their parents' objections to discussing such disturbing subject matter now when the world was so much more enlightened. Jennifer never forgot her teacher's reply, "It is important for you to see this and remember the barbarity we humans are capable of. Civilization is never more than one generation away from barbarism."

The memory dropped into her gut so heavily that her knees grew too weak to support her. She fell into the chair shaking.

Then a government official appeared on the screen. He was responding to questions about the asylum program that the cheerful journalist was asking him. Jennifer had missed most of what he said. She thought he looked uncomfortable. His name briefly flashed on the screen—Aaron Ger-something. She made herself pay attention. Could Ana possibly be detained as an asylum seeker? She had completed all the paperwork required months before she and Jennifer met and had been notified that she had been accepted. Detaining her would not make sense.

When the news anchor moved on to a celebrity scandal, Jennifer changed the channel. Another anchor person was discussing the crackdown throughout Europe on immigrants who come illegally claiming to be escaping persecution. It seemed to be tonight's "breaking news." Footage showed men hanging onto the underside of rail cars, risking their lives to cross the border from Spain into France. A reporter showed viewers the encampments of those caught near the Chunnel that carried freight and passengers under the English Channel from France to England. He showed where those apprehended lived—encampments of utter squalor where they slept in tents made of whatever they could find. Children in torn clothes and with no shoes begged the reporter for food. Mothers looking like grandmothers used their headscarves to cover their nursing babies. There were no men in sight.

Another channel showed angry crowds waving national flags in Berlin, Germany and Rome, Italy, in Budapest, Hungary and Warsaw, Poland. The reporter translated their chants into English: "Send them back" and "Lock them up."

She texted her Mum to turn their TV to Sky News. She knew her Dad would be mumbling the angry words he used increasingly these past four years since the Ultra-Right had won the election. Mum would be shaking her head in silent protest. Jennifer wondered about Damir and Mohammed. Were they safe here in this charged political climate?

She scribbled what she remembered of the name of the government official on the back of the professor's card. Then she washed up her dishes and retreated to her bed for another night of restless sleep.

CHAPTER 9

On her lunch hour Jennifer took the subway to the university stop, exited and walked to the chemical engineering building. She climbed the marble stairs to the entrance, went through the metal detector, then climbed to the third floor, finding door number 318. She knocked. When a deep baritone voice with an Arabic accent said, "Come in," she opened the door and entered. She was still trying to decide how to present herself. She must not endanger him by saying too much. They both were likely on the watch list. What could she say? She felt awkward and nervous and took overlong to speak.

"Professor, I am a prospective student interested in your advice as to which classes I should take next semester." It sounded lame even to her ears. Then, before he could reply and send her to the advisement office, she passed him a sheet of paper on which she had written a summary of Ana's disappearance.

"Won't you sit down," he said. "Just a minute while I finish up what I am working on." He read what she had passed him, then read it again, folded it up and returned it to her. "I haven't had my lunch today. Perhaps we could talk over a coffee in the cafeteria?"

"Of course. Thank you." They said nothing else until they were outside the building walking across the campus.

"They watch me closely. Did you notice the fellow behind us? He will have noted and photographed your visit. We don't have much time to talk…Your Ana's case is not unusual. I have been told of at least a dozen people who have disappeared in similar circumstances since January. They have cracked down on all immigrants since the election, but especially those with brown skins, hijabs, and home countries in North Africa and the Middle East. Have you contacted Amnesty International or Human Rights Watch?"

"Yes. They need more information to do anything other than keep her name in their databases."

"Of course. There are MPs who are monitoring this. Have you contacted them? Clare Harris-Alston or Sir Hugh Anderson, both in the New Independent Party. Or perhaps Donald MacKenzie, a new Labour Party MP from Glasgow, or Dame Edith Owens, also Labour and herself an institution? We've come to the cafeteria already. Can you give me your phone number in case I think of more? Now let's have some lunch and light conversation about you and your interest in chemical engineering." He smiled at her with a fatherly kindness and she struggled to maintain her composure. She had felt so isolated and unsafe. In just a few minutes she knew she could trust him.

Over the next thirty minutes he told her about his own career in chemical engineering, his education at Cambridge, his family members still in Pakistan. He asked her about her interest in the field. Of course, she made things up--a friend who has made a successful career in chemical engineering, the opportunity to consult with other governments and work on projects abroad, an interest since childhood in how things work. Listening to herself she thought she wasn't half bad at this. Then lunch was over. She thanked him and crossed the campus to the Tube stop. When she looked back, she saw the man who had been following them was moving across the campus a discrete distance behind Professor Zafar.

CHAPTER 10

Ana was a freelance journalist. Consequently, she belonged to no one media outlet. She sold her stories to a variety of papers and online magazines. Jennifer had tried to locate professional colleagues who might have ideas about where Ana was. One man, a young, long-haired Brit from Essex, told Jennifer he knew that Ana was working on a story about asylum seekers and how the UK was handling them. He thought she had discovered an important lead, but he knew no more than that. Jennifer had already known that much, but Ana was fiercely protective of her sources and shared little if anything about what she was finding with anyone, even Jennifer. "I need to protect you from being involved with this," she had told Jennifer the week before she disappeared. "What I am learning is really important, a big story, and something I must pursue on my own."

That conversation and the news coverage of asylum percolated in Jennifer's mind during the following week, along with the names of MPs suggested by Professor Zafar. But her job kept her too busy to do anything else until Friday. She must act this week while the asylum story was fresh. She called in to her office Friday morning and pleaded sickness to get a day off that she could devote to following up with the MPs. That required a trip to Whitehall.

Jennifer was not a particularly political person, although the last election had grabbed her attention. The victory of the Ultra-Right was a first in British history and matched similar victories across Europe, in Hungary, Austria, Germany, Spain, Portugal, Greece, and France and in the United States. She went to the library before taking the Tube to Whitehall. She used the internet and library computers there to look up the four MPs the professor had suggested. It was safer than using the internet at home.

Sir Hugh Anderson had a seat on the Homeland Security committee. Dame Edith Owens was a member of the committee that dealt with refugees and asylum. Clare Harris-Alston, New Independent Party, was outspokenly critical of the new government's immigration policy, especially its treatment of Middle Easterners. She was the daughter of a former ambassador to Jordan and had grown up in the Middle East as her father moved through a series of diplomatic assignments there. Her committee dealt with child welfare. Donald MacKenzie? It wasn't evident to her from the quick research she did why he was on Professor Zafar's list. He sat on Government Oversight and appeared to be a new member of that committee. She found several articles online highlighting his strong verbal criticisms of government spending that was inadequately and misleadingly documented and another article on his involvement in working against climate change. She decided to start with Dame Edith.

By the time she reached the offices of Parliament it was nearing early afternoon. Dame Edith was, of course, unavailable. She was attending a hearing of the Committee on Asylum, her secretary told Jennifer. "It is open to the public if you wish to go. Perhaps you can have a word with her at the end."

Jennifer's footsteps echoed as she walked down the long marble hallway looking for the hearing room. She felt quite uncomfortable in this world of powerful people who had little time for ordinary folks like her, but she forced herself to open the heavy wooden door and enter the hearing room. MPs sat at a dais looking down on the person testifying below them. Jennifer thought he looked familiar. She squeezed past a row of spectators to reach the one remaining empty seat and sank into it with relief. Perhaps she would look inconspicuous among these others watching what before she would have called a boring hearing. Now, however, she sat up straight and listened carefully, pulling a pen and a small spiral notebook from her handbag to make notes.

On the dais a white-haired woman with an intense look leaned into the microphone and spoke to the man sitting before them. "And when did you visit the asylum camp? Can you please tell us what you saw there? Please don't leave out details." Her voice was authoritative, the voice of a woman accustomed to exercising power.

Jennifer wondered what course the woman's life had taken to bring her to this place. Then she refocused on what the man was saying. He spoke slowly, like he was searching for words, wanting to be careful, cautious. "The women, children and men are housed in separate barracks. The women are employed doing small electronics assembly. The men pulverize stone to make a substance used to waterproof wood. That is what I was told. The children are housed separately, and I was told they receive lessons in English and other school subjects. They see their mothers only for the evening meal. It seemed very orderly, regimented, sterile, and the armed guards watching over the women while they worked seemed excessive to me."

"Did you interview any of those held at the camp?"

"Not individually. My escort said that was not permitted. I spoke with a small group of men and another small group of women."

"You were there as a government official, were you not?"

The witness looked increasingly uncomfortable. His face was ruddy and his eyes avoided meeting the penetrating stare of his interrogator. "Yes and no, madam. I went because I wanted to understand why the appropriation for refugees and asylum seekers had increased so noticeably. My boss gave me permission to go. He did not instruct me to go."

The white-haired woman smiled and leaned back in her chair. "Well, that is very commendable of you, sir. Watching out for His Majesty's expenditures, were you." A soft murmur of laughter rolled across the chamber. When it subsided, she continued. "And did what you learned you satisfy your concerns?"

"Yes, madam. The eight meter concrete wall, the considerable new construction of additional barracks as far as the eye can see, also happening in other camp locations, the vast number of new people assigned to the camps—I believe that could explain the tripling of the appropriation requested." He continued to avoid her eyes and the eyes of others seated on the dais.

"Is there anything else you wish to share with us today? Remember, we are very interested in what is happening to these asylum seekers."

There was a pause while he sat looking at the papers in front of him. Then he raised his eyes to look directly at her and said in a stronger voice, "I would like to consult my notes and get back with you if I find anything, madam."

She seemed startled to see him suddenly forceful. "Of course. My assistant will give you my card, sir. I hope to hear from you."

The man shrank back into his mild mannered, milk-toast bureaucrat mode, and the remainder of the hearing was taken up by other members of the committee asking detailed questions about line items in the appropriations request. Jennifer tuned out. Instead she observed the white-haired woman and the witness before them. At four o'clock the witness was dismissed, and the committee disbanded for the day. Members departed through a door behind the dais rather than using the one Jennifer had entered.

Jennifer scrambled over the knees of the people seated beside her murmuring "Sorry... sorry... sorry" and made her exit, following the hall back to Dame Edith's office.

"Oh, you just missed her, miss. She's meeting someone in her office now. Not sure how long it will take. Why not leave a note for her with your concern? She is good about getting back to constituents."

Jennifer took a seat and worried over the note she would write. After a while she wrote, "Dear Dame Edith, I have a close friend who is a journalist writing about asylum seekers. Perhaps you have read her pieces, Ana Amara? She disappeared nearly four months ago. I am desperate to find her, and you are my best hope. I believe she was being watched by the Security Services, as am I probably. I know this may sound crazy. Please, can we talk?" She wrote her office phone number and extension after her name, folded the note and placed it in an envelope that she sealed before passing it to the receptionist. "Please make sure Dame Edith reads this herself, not just her staff." She spoke in a whisper and the receptionist noted the stricken look on the young woman's face as she turned and left the office.

CHAPTER 11

Aaron Geronsky left Dame Edith's office after five p.m. By then the phalanx if media had dispersed and the offices were closing for the day. He didn't want to be recognized exiting Dame Edith's office. His decision to speak with her in chambers was spur of the moment, made without forethought and fueled by the memories of his conversation with the women at the camp and the pitiful note in blood on toilet tissue. He hadn't known what to do with that information. Clearly his boss was not interested in anything that might rock the boat. Like so many career government workers, the advent of the Ultra government made him excessively anxious that his position in the foreign service might be jeopardized. He had confided to Aaron that, with a daughter at uni and a son waiting to hear if he was accepted into government service, one couldn't be too careful.

Dame Edith, by contrast, appeared to really be interested in the truth. The truth he would tell her, unlike anything revealed in public hearings, was certainly interesting. Troubling, too. Very troubling. Consequently, he had followed her to her office where, when she recognized him, she had ushered him quickly into her inner sanctum. She seemed to understand that this meek man, who had testified before her committee and suddenly come to life when he asked if he could get her answers at a later time, had something he needed to say in private. She listened as he recounted the women's candid comments about being imprisoned and separated from their husbands and children, about being beaten. Dame Edith looked closely at the photo on his cell phone of a wrinkled piece of toilet tissue with squiggly brown letters that spelled HELP.

When he was finished, she walked him to the unmarked door from her office suite, thanking him for providing her this important information. As the door closed behind him, her eye caught an envelope to which was stuck a bright pink sticky-pad note marked "Dame Edith—eyes only. " She carried it with her as she returned to her inner office and sank down on the leather sofa, kicking off her high heels. She uttered a long, audible sigh that said, had anyone been there to hear it, that this job was, on days like today, taxing and troubling. Then she opened the envelope and read Jennifer's note.

Aaron Geronsky's phone rang while he was on the Tube heading home to Marissa and the twins. It was Dame Edith. Her message was cryptic, suspecting her phone might also be tapped. "Would you recognize her?"

"Recognize whom?"

"The woman with the toilet tissue."

"No. I saw only her covered head."

"All right then. Cheers." She clicked off.

There was a message waiting for him when he arrived home. It had come on their landline and was from his boss. It, too, was succinct to the point of abruptness. "Aaron, complaints from upstairs about your testimony. Tread carefully."

Aaron thought this caution might be coming too late.

CHAPTER 12

Dame Edith used her private line to phone her colleagues, "the Gang of Four," they called themselves jokingly. Donald MacKenzie was still in Glasgow on family business, returning tomorrow. Clare Harris-Ashton was at her home in North London. It was, after all, Friday evening. But Hugh Anderson, bless him, was still in the building. A typical workaholic and possibly an alcoholic as well, he rarely arrived home before nine. Dame Edith had speculated that he might not be keen about his wife of twenty-three years. Certainly Dame Edith wasn't keen on her. She pondered half a minute and then asked him to come to her office. "Sounds rather cloak and dagger," he replied. "Or maybe you're ready to give up your long-touted celibacy to a handsome, brilliant, graying peer who's as dedicated to slaying dragons as you yourself?" he teased.

"Why don't you come and see?" she replied saucily. They had long been friends, the kind that teased each other but also listened to each other. The kind that are rare in public life. She set out the sherry and cheeses with biscuits—MPs who kept her hours stocked their offices with food to get them through these long nights, as well as blankets and pillows for when they were too tired to go home. She kept a duplicate set of clothes and make up in her office toilet and spent the night in her office probably once a week.

Hugh arrived hale and hearty and gave her a kiss in greeting. She noted that he seemed quite happy to have been invited. Poor man, probably looking for anything to avoid going home. She threw a grateful thought to Dennis, the love of her life and her husband for thirty-five years, until pancreatic cancer took him three years ago. While Dennis was alive she never welcomed late nights at the office. But that was then. Now late nights were a distraction from the quiet emptiness of their house just off Hampstead Heath, although walking their cocker spaniel, Dodger, on the Heath provided both exercise and a break from her loneliness. Funny how getting out around other people on a stroll, even when you knew no one and had no interest in getting to know them, lifted the gloom. Even when the city itself was in the doldrums, dripping rain and depression for days on end, Dennis would say, "It's the exercise that lifts your spirits, dearie, that and our darling dog."

When she and Hugh had settled at opposite ends of the long sofa with their sherries and cheese, she told him about Aaron Geronsky's visit to a camp for those seeking asylum. Then she passed him Jennifer's note.

"Good Lord! What are we running here? A reprise of the 1940s?" Hugh exclaimed. She loved his passion. You could count on it even in times like these when so many progressives were remaining silent or modifying their responses to sound "even handed" and "moderate." "I remember Ana Amara's articles. Sometimes *The Guardian* published her. Always thoughtful. You could count on her to turn up new information and analyze it with care. She'd been writing about those seeking asylum, as I recall but for several months there have been no more articles under her byline. But, disappeared?"

"The appropriation for refugees and asylum seekers has yet to be voted out of committee. That means we still have leverage, it seems to me. We can demand access to the camps and lists of those held there. We can send a delegation of MPs there to take a careful look and, only after all of that is accomplished, take a vote on the appropriation." Dame Edith's voice was low and calculated. She had been in Parliament long enough to know how a small group, like the Gang of Four, could magnify its influence by taking advantage of the legislative calendar. Timing was key.

"Homeland Security is also in hearings next week. Perhaps we need to learn who is being flown into the camps and why and from what countries they are coming. Damn, 150 countries are a hell of a lot. Can we really have asylum seekers from 150 countries or are they using a different definition of asylum, perhaps including people from any country where terrorists have struck?"

"All right, then. We will convene the Gang of Four for first thing Monday and see what each of us can do."

The old friends continued chatting, trading ideas for a while, then settled into more personal conversation. It was difficult in politics to be candid with colleagues, but they had been working in Westminster for a long time and had discovered in each other true comradeship. They could test ideas, discuss their peers, share frustrations and obsessions with full confidence that what was said would not reach the ears of others. Theirs was true friendship, increasingly rare in a country undergoing seismic political shifts that were carrying it farther and farther into uncharted territory. They both believed what was going on was anathema to democracy and were not afraid to say so. Friendship like this compensated for having little to go home to.

The following Monday the Gang of Four met in Clare Harris-Alston's inner office promptly at eight in the morning. Dame Edith briefed them on Aaron Geronsky's testimony and his confidential conversation with her afterwards. She showed them Jennifer's note, and caught them up on her conversation with Hugh. Together they came up with a plan.

Dame Edith would circulate a letter to her committee stating the need to delay voting on the appropriation for refugees and asylum seekers until members of the committee had visited the burgeoning asylum camps and interviewed residents.

Hugh, who had the highest security clearance among them, would ask the leading Tory on Homeland Security to join him in requesting an off-the-record briefing from the head of Homeland Security. Together they would ask for a list of those interned and for plans for their release. They would specifically subpoena information on children being held, names, numbers, where they were held, daily activities, dates of admittance to the camps, amount of parental contact. While he would be sworn to secrecy about what he learned, Hugh could look for Ana's name and could advise his colleagues what locations to personally visit as part of their investigation.

Once that meeting took place, Clare would request the Child Welfare committee she served on to hold hearings with organizations that assist refugees. This would provide documentation of their situation and attract media attention to their plight. Among those testifying would be MPs who were part of Dame Edith's investigation team, those who had first-hand information from visiting a camp. Children's Day in the UK was less than a month away. They would hold the hearings then to maximize media coverage. Dame Edith, with another peer she would recruit to visit the camps, would take the press to the concrete walled internment camp Aaron Geronsky had visited. The optics alone would be striking—"protecting" asylum seekers by detaining them in a virtual prison that resembled Hitler's concentration camps.

Donald MacKenzie sat facing the carpet while Dame Edith summarized their assignments. He had none. "I feel a mite useless," he said apologetically.

"I thought you mentioned once that you had a university chum who is in MI-6?" Trust Hugh to always be helpful, Dame Edith thought to herself. "Why not have a pint with him and chat him up about the atmosphere there among his colleagues? It would help to know where we might find allies within the secret services. Is he someone who might find incarcerating children of refugees distressing? Better yet, what about your former colleagues at university? Surely there are some Pakis and Syrians you could sound out about what their communities are experiencing?"

"I don't know. Haven't seen my MI-6 friend in several years, but I'll think about who I can talk with in my old department."

Donald was a chemistry don by training, drawn to run for a seat in the Commons by his distress over the direction the country had taken, especially abandoning the fight against global warming. He was new, still a bit uncertain about his role in the Commons, but a man whose convictions led him to give up a high position in academia in exchange for a thankless job amid the current chaos of Parliament. His tentative smile showed how grateful he was to be included and, despite his inexperience, assigned a task.

CHAPTER 13

Professor Ibrahim arrived at the mosque for evening prayers weary and worried. At first, he'd been paralyzed by depression after receiving the news that he would not be granted tenure. Without tenure, he had to find employment elsewhere within the next year. Then he had pushed himself into overdrive, putting out feelers to a dozen other universities. But he had received no responses. He supposed he could try community colleges. They were always searching for PhDs who would work for a pittance. What if they, too, were afflicted with fear of Muslims? What then? He had a wife and two children to support, not to mention his parents back home in Syria who needed his monthly cash transfers to live in their retirement.

His mouth tasted as sour as his disposition, and he washed his hands and face, nostrils and mouth with special diligence trying to alter the state of his mind and body. He would go before Allah in prayer with a clean heart and mind. There were fewer than a dozen men at prayers this night. He liked it when the group was small. It felt intimate. They might be few, but their faith was mighty and would see them through whatever rough times lay ahead. His prayers this night were especially fervent and he welcomed the calm they brought to his soul.

A week later Professor Ibrahim had still received no positive response to his applications to universities and community colleges. It was mid-October and he was beginning to panic. The rumors he overheard as he left the mosque after prayers that night multiplied his anxiety. The men were talking about some

Muslims who had been living legally in the community who had been seized during the night and had disappeared. He intensified scanning the internet, obsessively reading any advertisements for positions in chemical engineering.

When he checked his university mailbox one crisp autumn morning, he found a plain envelope with no marking other than his name in the address space. He slid his finger along the flap to open the envelope and found a folded newsprint ad for a position at a private university in Devon. The school specialized in animal husbandry yet was seeking a chemical engineer. According the ad, "We seek someone to staff a grant we have received to research low-tech chemical explosives, the kind that might be simply manufactured in Afghanistan or Central Asia." He wondered if his department chair might have put the ad in his box, feeling guilty about denying him tenure. He looked up the location on Google Map—nearly five hours by car from London in the middle of pastoral east England, one of the least populated regions in the UK.

His current research had no connection to explosives, but before he left Syria he had been employed by the Assad government to research chemical weapons. The lab he worked in was doing preventive research, they were told, studying how to equip and train the Syrian army to protect them from the simple yet lethal chemical weapons guerrilla groups might manufacture from easily obtainable insecticides.

The memory of the day that changed his life washed over him now, and he stood and began pacing his small office, back and forth, anxiety flooding through him. He would never forget the details of that day. He had been standing in the lab chatting with his colleagues about the World Cup when a news report came across the television from BBC. It said that the Assad government had used chemical weapons on Syrian civilians.

His president had betrayed him, betrayed them all. He had begun shaking and had to sit down. He had telephoned Amra and told her to collect the children and be ready to leave in one hour. He deleted his files, cleaned out his office, and fled, collecting Amra and their children, and arriving at the British Embassy, to ask, beg, plead for asylum.

Because of his prominent position, the Brits let the family enter the Embassy and paved the way for all of them to get to the UK. He had been very fortunate.

The two chemical engineers he had been talking football with when that broadcast came across the airwaves had also attempted to flee. A few days later in the room assigned to his family in the British Embassy he watched a television report of their public executions. He pulled Amra toward him and covered her eyes when he realized that what they were seeing on the screen were photos of their friends' mangled bodies.

Now in his small office at the university he could not shake these memories. Once the British arranged their transport out of Syria to London, he kept his past inside him. He had told no one he met in the UK of his previous work or of his sudden flight from Syria. No one but Amra knew—although he supposed the British secret services knew.

He could not concentrate. The anonymous job advert did not help. He had vowed never again to do research that would, even could, result in weapons of mass destruction. Worrying about the future churned and soured his stomach.

At three he decided he had to ask for help. He phoned a colleague, a Brit with whom he played on a local football team. The weariness in his voice must have alarmed his friend, who suggested they meet in half an hour for a coffee or a pint.

The Black Horse Pub was one block from campus. They chose a quiet unpopulated corner in the back and sipped their drinks silently. His friend did not want to rush him, so he tolerated the silence and waited until Ibrahim was ready to talk. Slowly Ibrahim's story seeped out, not the story of his life in Syria but the story of his life here at this university—how hard he had worked to attain tenure, the chair's abrupt rejection of his tenure application, the absence of interest from any of the universities and colleges he had contacted, his growing panic that he might not be able to support his family in this time when Islamophobia was receiving support from the highest levels of the government. When he finished his litany of woes, his friend sat silent. He seemed to be reviewing the job options he was aware of, problem solving. Finally, he said two words: Porton Downs.

"It's a well-respected but secret facility that began in World War I after chemical weapons were used by Germany on British troops. It's the lab that established that Assad was using sarin on his own people. You remember?"

Of course, Ibrahim remembered.

"Their research is preventative—preparing soldiers to be invulnerable to chemical attacks. I've heard they employ nearly three thousand people. A notice came through my email today that they are hiring more, part of the Ultra's expansion of military weapons R&D. I'll forward it to you. I know you want to teach, but your experience in Syria would make you a most attractive candidate, I suspect."

His reference to Ibrahim's work in Syria startled Ibrahim. What did he know? What did his department know? Did his peers here identify him as some sort of evil agent of Asaad's terror?

His friend continued spinning out possibilities. He hadn't noticed Ibrahim's alarm. "Also, the University of Glasgow just received a research grant to their chemical engineering program. You could check it out as well. Look, Ibrahim, you're a brilliant scientist. You have so much to offer any program, and it might be that being Syrian could be an added credential for some positions like weapons research."

He was probably right, although Ibrahim had vowed he would never again do weapons research. "Preventive chemical weapons research"—that's also what the Asaad government had called his work for them. How could you be certain what your research would be used for?

Could he conduct military research for any country? Yet how else would he provide for his family? His friend had named some options, at least. That was helpful, though he feared where they might lead.

Before they parted, the two colleagues embraced. They had never done that before. His friend had walked back his despair and given him hope, however slim. He had to express his gratitude for that, for his friend listening to him and for his suggestions. In Syria men showing such affection was routine, but he had seen few men hugging in Britain. He hoped he had not overstepped.

As he got into his car, his hand, reaching for his keys, happened on the folded piece of newsprint with the job advert at that rural university. In his current state of mind, such a remote, rural location sounded safer than living here southeast of London.

CHAPTER 14

On the weekend, when he returned to his home in Glasgow, Donald MacKenzie met with a former colleague from his student days who was now a professor in the chemistry department at the University of Glasgow. His former friend, well aware of Donald's professional success and of his new career in Parliament, pontificated about the grants available to chemical engineers willing to do military research—much more money there than in pharma research, he told Donald. A colleague known to them both had altered his research program and written a grant to research how to counter the devastating effect of binary nerve gas, the chemical weapons used by Syria's President Assad.

"He is rolling in grant money, the clever chap. He's riding the Ultra tidal wave. One needs not only the scientific background but the savvy to sniff the wind and identify which direction the geyser of grants is flowing, and with the Ultras in power, military research money—especially chemical research—is gushing. Everyone in the sciences knows those willing to turn these tricks whether it has been their field of speciality or not. You might consider it. I'm sure it would pay much more than an MPs salary, Donald." The man gave him a wink and a conspiratorial smile.

The conversation made Donald quite uncomfortable, and he abruptly changed its direction.

"Say, do you know any professors in chemical engineering from the Middle East? Of course, there are large numbers of international students from Middle Eastern countries studying engineering—industrial, mechanical, chemical. And many of them—once they earn their PhDs—remain here teaching, but I'm rather out of the loop since the last election. Do you know any of these chaps? I'm assuming they're likely to be male."

"Not necessarily. There are some stellar female chemists from the Middle East, too." The professor from the University of Glasgow was intrigued by Donald's question. "Why are you interested?"

Donald mumbled something vague about a Parliamentary committee interested in doing a longitudinal study on the contribution of immigrants and he'd thought, as a chemical engineer himself, he'd like to include people in his field. It was a weak explanation and he knew it as soon as the words left his mouth. To cover he asked a quick follow up. "Have you any in your department?"

"Two, although I don't really know them. They stay to themselves. I do have a classmate teaching at Uni Sussex in the aban I could put you in touch with him. Nice chap. Young, more diligent than most of these ragheads, and no jihadist. He looks normal enough, and I can talk with him about those dangerous clowns pillaging the region with their packs of C-4 and those invading this country. He seems to quite agree with me. I don't buy your reason for looking for Pakis and Saudis—you're probably doing something clandestine—but as a true patriot, I'll not probe." He fumbled with his mobile phone and brought up a contact. "I just texted you the contact information of the professor."

After that their conversation rambled through how each family was and where they were planning to travel over the summer holiday. When it started into politics, especially the Scottish Nationalist Party's recent coalition with the ruling Ultras, Donald checked his phone and attempted to look regretful as he said he was late for another appointment and must go. The man's politics troubled him.

On the Monday when he returned to London, Donald called the man at Uni Sussex and set up a time to meet. He suggested a popular pub near the campus. Only after he rang off did he realize he had made a cultural faux pas. As a Muslim the professor probably did not drink alcohol. Oh, well, he decided, not wanting to ring him back and call attention to his cultural insensitivity. Surely there will be something he can eat and drink there.

CHAPTER 15

There was no denying that the woman in Barrack #7 was pregnant. Several other women in that barrack had been pregnant and, when their time came, were assisted by the other women to deliver their babies. The births brought transitory moments of joy and connection to the women. It was delightful to watch the new mothers cuddling and nursing their little ones and the other women attempting to be helpful. Births were a reminder that life goes on, that there is another dimension rooted more deeply than the experience of incarceration, an ancient dimension that connects human kind in all times and places.

The tall black woman named Mali was a midwife in her other life, her life other than here. She took the lead helping the women give birth and showed them how to help the baby latch onto their nipples. She encouraged those whose milk was slow to drop and praised their small, mewing babies. "Everyone deserves to be celebrated at their birth," she would say.

Two babies were born within the same week to asylum mothers in Barrack 7. One evening six weeks later they were not brought into the barrack to nurse. The matron said that they were being switched to formula to make less work for their mothers. When they did not come a second night, their mothers were nearly frantic to see them, fearful that something terrible may have happened to their babies. The matron was reassuring, but night three brought no babies. By night four, the eldest of the two bereft mothers was wailing and tearing at her clothes, sobbing that she must see her child. She had lost two children to the bombing in the Syrian war, and her grief was wild and agonizing to witness. The matron summoned help and had her carried away, no one knew where. Neither she nor the babies returned.

The second mother, fearing the same outcome, stifled her grief. They could hear her at night crying. They could hear, too, the percussive beat of the metal legs of her bed hitting the floor, left side and then right, left and then right, as she rocked herself to sleep. Her grief filled the air like dust motes they could not avoid breathing in.

Mali encouraged the last remaining pregnant woman in their barrack to have faith and trust that Allah would not abandon her. He would make a way out of no way. It was his promise.

From the night of the first birth Mali had noticed a younger woman standing with the others, her eyes intent as though she was taking in every detail. She had squeezed one hand into a fist and pounded it against her chest. "We are here and we will not forget," she whispered to Mali. But she had been moved from Barrack #7.

CHAPTER 16

It required two weeks to arrange a delegation visit to the camp in Devon. MPs on the Child Welfare Committee would agree to join the delegation and then, when they learned it meant driving five hours one way to Devon, they would back off. Final permission was required from the cabinet Secretary for Immigration and Refugees for the delegation to enter the camp. It did not come until several days before the planned visit. In the end four MPs made the trip, all of them women.

The Secretary's excuse for the delay was that she had been busy finalizing the New Asylum Accommodation and Support Services Contracts (AASC) that the Home Office awarded to three private companies. A fortune could be made through these contracts. The government was giving four billion pounds to these three private corporations over ten years. The Secretary had a copy of her press release delivered to Dame Edith's office to pacify Dame Edith. It read: "The UK has a proud history of providing protection to those who need it and these new contracts will make sure that asylum seekers are treated with dignity and respect in safe, secure and suitable accommodation....They will deliver compassionate support through a new integrated service and make the asylum system more accessible and easier to navigate...."

Such Bollocks. Dame Edith's disgust was evident in her words and facial expression. "They claim they've consulted extensively with local authorities and non-government organizations to make sure that the contracts protect vulnerable asylum seekers as well as delivering value for the taxpayers' money directed to pay for their management of the camps. It's nothing but Bollocks!" In a moment of rare anger she tossed the press release onto the floor and stomped from her outer into her inner office.

While they awaited confirmation of the date of their visit, Clare worked to persuade the chair of her Child Welfare Committee to hold a hearing on November 20—Children's Day. The day before they departed for the asylum camp Dame Edith and the other two women accompanying her and Clare received invitations to testify at that hearing. Dame Edith phoned Jennifer to tell her the good news and to assure her they would be visiting the camp, only one of at least half a dozen camps. They would do their best to get information about Ana Amara.

Theirs was not the first delegation from Parliament to investigate the camps. Nearly a decade earlier an investigation by Andrew Shale had turned up a rather damning report on the treatment of refugees that called attention to the number of people "at risk" of dread diseases who were detained in the camps. That report stimulated some reforms. Shale had recommended limitations on the time one could be detained and giving special care to the elderly, the weak, and children, all those who would "suffer disproportionate detriment from being detained …and therefore [were] unsuitable for immigration detention" without compelling evidence of criminality. One camp had been closed and another relocated. It appeared the Shale report was having some effect, although his follow up report in 2018 found that though his policy recommendations had been approved by the government, the same circumstances were still normative. Then the 2021 election—after Britain left the European Union, shaking its economy—the new nationalist party, the Ultras, had come to power. The Ultras had no tolerance for immigrants, asylum seekers or "sniveling liberals" like Andrew Shale. That had been the beginning of the changes that Dame Edith believed were making Great Britain, the cradle of democracy, unrecognizable.

When the required permissions were finally delivered to Dame Edith's office, the delegation set out in a government car with a driver to see for themselves just how Britain under Ultra leadership was treating its asylum seekers.

Hugh's effort to get Homeland Security to provide him with a list of those detained failed utterly. He contacted a half-dozen human rights groups to enlist their aid locating Ana Amara, and, on their advice, he asked Homeland Security if Ana Amara, was among those in detention. Homeland Security answered that a woman by that name was in asylum detention. Hugh asked his contact there for a photo of the woman by that name who was detained. His contact stonewalled him for ten days. The delegation's visit was hours away, when Homeland Security delivered an envelope to Hugh's office with a grainy black and white profile photo of a pregnant woman wearing a burqa and hijab. Written on the back was "Ana Amara."

CHAPTER 17

The women at the Devon camp did not talk as they assembled small digital devices in the large warehouse. It was what they did every week day and Saturday, but today was not like all the other days after all. Over a loud speaker came the voice of a tall man in a brown uniform who stood on a platform in front of them. His words were brief and surprising. "Tomorrow the camp will be visited by four Members of Parliament. I expect all of you to be polite, orderly and attentive to your tasks. Making a good impression on the MPs will ensure continued good treatment. You will be on your best behavior."

He appeared not to notice the current of energy that ran through the assembled women. His voice grew stronger and resonated with a timbre of irritation. "You are here under the kind treatment of His Majesty's Government. I remind you not to forget this." He waited while his words were translated into Arabic, Farsi, French, and Erdu by four young men also dressed in brown. Then he and they turned and exited the hall. The steel door clanged shut behind them.

That evening the pregnant woman in Barrack #7 was called to the matron's desk near the entryway. The matron did not look up from her paperwork. "You will be seeing a doctor regarding your pregnancy tomorrow while the MPs are visiting the camp. Please be sure you are clean for your examination."

As she walked back to her cot the young woman seethed with anger. How dare the matron suggest that I am unclean? Washing ourselves before we pray five times a day is part of our religion!

She must talk to Mali. If they are clever and lucky they may be able to get information to the MPs. They are allowed no paper other than toilet tissue so she hid some of the thin sheets in the folds of her burqa as she exited the toilet. This time she bit the pad of her middle finger until it started to bleed. Then she wrote in her own blood one word, all she had time for before the matron made a bed check and clicked off the lights.

In the dark after the matron locked them in, she conferred with Mali and passed her the tissue. Mali agreed to pass the tissue to one of the MPs, if she could get anywhere near them.

CHAPTER 18

The next evening Aaron Geronsky sat with his family watching television. A TV newscast was playing and Marissa had called him to come watch. "I think that woman is the MP you met with after your testimony, Aaron." Dame Edith and three other female MPs stood in front of the television cameras. A pounding rain complete with thunder nearly drowned out what they were saying. Listening closely he could make out that they had just visited a camp in Devon for asylum seekers. "The camp is run by a private business that has a contract with the Home Office to manage detention centers throughout England and Scotland," the reporter said, "and senior personnel at this facility are retired military, many having served in Iraq and/or Afghanistan. They allowed no photos to be taken." She asks the MPs she is interviewing to describe the place.

Cameras follow the high concrete wall topped with coils of razor wire that surrounds the camp, presumably to dissuade anyone from attempting to leave. The MPs say they were permitted to interview eight women, one each from Mali, Syria, Pakistan, Malaysia, Bangladesh, Nigeria, Sudan, and Kazakhstan. They describe the women as nervous, reluctant to say much. Their matron was standing within earshot. They did tell the MPs that they saw their children only once a day and that two women had delivered babies in the barracks where they lodged and that....

A brazen crack of thunder erased their words at that point and the reporter concluded her coverage of the interview.

The following morning *The Guardian* included an important detail that Aaron read with great interest. Apparently one MP was passed a torn piece of toilet tissue with the word HELP written in browned blood. Aaron's heart raced as he read the article. Could it be the same woman who had passed him the HELP tissue? Who is she and what does her desperate attempt to be known mean?

CHAPTER 19

In the Devon camp the following morning Officer Pendleton assembled the women who were interviewed. They stood in a line outside the warehouse squinting against the full sun. He was red-faced, tight-lipped and clearly unhappy. He stood like a piece of rebar, his large sunglasses hiding his eyes.

His voice was hard as steel. "Which of you passed you the paper?"

There was no response.

"Who?"

Silence.

"I will find you if you don't confess and you will be placed in corrective detention—solitary confinement."

He selected from the group the most regal woman, the tall brown woman from Mali. He stood too close to her and peered at her contemptuously.

"Are you the one?"

She simply stared back at him, head high, eyes half-hooded by defiance or by the glare, he could not tell which.

"Take her to the closet," he ordered his assistant.

CHAPTER 20

At his office in Westminster Hugh examined the photo of the woman who Homeland Security identified as Ana Amara. It was taken full length. There was no mistaking her swollen body. The face was in profile and obscured by the shadows cast by her hijab. When his assistant enlarged it and ran it through face recognition software, three photos of different women appeared to be possible matches. He called an emergency meeting of the Gang of Four in his office to see the photos, and Dame Edith called Jennifer to come to Westminster to try to make an identification.

Jennifer left work immediately. She barely noticed that her boss gave her an annoyed look. She took the Tube to Westminster and walked quickly to Hugh's office. Seated at Sir Hugh's desk she studied the computer screen, which showed three women, each with the same name, each detained. As Dame Edith, Clare Harris-Ashton and Donald MacKenzie entered Sir Hugh's office, they heard Hugh ask Jennifer, "Do you know any of these women?"

"Yes. The one in the middle is my Ana." There was a collective sigh of relief.

Next Hugh showed her the profile photo taken in the detention center. "Is this Ana?"

"I can't tell, her face is out of focus. But Ana would never be pregnant."

"Why do you say that?"

His question made her uncomfortable. She did not want to violate their agreement to keep their relationship to themselves. Ana was a very private person and being a lesbian was viewed as evil, haram, and to be punished among some groups of Muslims as it was among some groups of Christians. They had pledged to keep their relationship covert to protect Ana. Jennifer chose her words carefully.

"If this woman is Ana, something terrible must have happened to her. She has never slept with a man." Is her answer ambiguous enough? She continued, "She would not be pregnant, not by her choice, not with her consent."

"The photo Jennifer has selected from the three identified by face recognition software is of Ana Amara," Hugh explained to the other three MPs. "And the photo supplied by SmartSecurity they claim is her as well, although Jennifer insists Ana never had sexual relations with a man and therefore could not be pregnant, and this woman is definitely pregnant." Hugh was struggling to understand how this could be and speculating out loud. "Might she have been raped in punishment for her 'crime' of sexual identity? We hear of honor killings and honor rapes. Might this explain her condition?"

How did they know? Jennifer had been so discrete, so careful not to expose the nature of her relationship with Ana to protect Ana. If this—or these—MPs knew, who else knew? Could she have been punished because she loves me? Dismayed and alarmed, Jennifer decided not to respond to his question.

"Can we subpoena her and have a closed session interview with her to protect her?" Clare Harris-Ashton suggested.

"I doubt we can subpoena an inmate of the camp, but we can subpoena the director of the Devon camp," Dame Edith responded.

Their questions and ideas tumbled over each other, coming too rapidly for Donald MacKenzie to add his voice. Hugh turned to Jennifer. "Can you be free to testify on Wednesday?"

"Won't I place her in more danger by testifying?"

"We must get this story out to the people of the UK. They won't stand for this." Hugh was insistent. He was not averse to using the power of his office to intimidate this reluctant young woman.

Dame Edith leaned against the bookshelves that lined her office walls. "Hugh, you have more faith in the British people than I have. Today many of them would wonder why books lined the walls of this office! Few of my constituents read books. Most rely on the internet for their information and, for the past few years, the internet has been controlled by those who can buy cloud space, web addresses and social media sites." She thought but did not say, Jennifer is right to be afraid. The media can be manipulated and "truth" molded to fit any special interest. A young Muslim woman who covers and who is a lesbian? Not a likely candidate for public sympathy these days. She hoped she had not gotten this poor girl and her partner into deeper water. The undertow is strong, and whomever has the money to flood these outlets controls the tide and carries the people.

CHAPTER 21

They had both expected more from life when they had fled Syria for Britain, but jobs for refugees tended to be those that paid in cash and involved no paperwork. Damir delivered pizzas, and Mohammed washed dishes at a Mediterranean restaurant in SoHo despite having taken some courses at a university. By combining their earnings they could pay for a one-room apartment. But the isolation of their life in London was depressing. No one took the time to exchange greetings and ask about your family. You signed in and signed out of work and might go the whole day without exchanging words with your coworkers. At least Mohammed had a more predictable schedule than Damir, which he appreciated. Most nights he returned from work about midnight after washing the floor of the restaurant and setting the tables and chairs for the next day's customers who would start arriving at ten in the morning.

Mohammed was the eldest brother, the middle child of those who had survived. Damir was three years younger, seventeen, the baby of the family. Mohammed felt responsible for him, especially now that it was only the two of them, now that Ana had made her crazy choice to mix outward and visible signs of her religion with a satanic Western life style that no imam would find acceptable.

On this Saturday night as he walked his weary body to their apartment, Mohammed noticed a man he had seen leaving the mosque had exited the subway at the same stop. He was walking a few meters behind Mohammed and then moved closer so that they were side by side for the last ten meters to the boys' apartment. They exchanged greetings, shook hands and chatted in Arabic about nothing important until they reached the apartment. Then they parted with the greeting of peace, "As-Salaam Alekum"—"Alekum Salaam."

The following night the man again appeared and the night after that. He appeared to be older than Mohammed, although not by much. They spoke little as the time they walked together was short. Both used the respectful form of speech one uses with an elder or a superior. Their greetings were formulaic but they had the flavor of home. Mohammed began to look for him.

After a week of these daily coincidental meetings, the man suggested they go for a coffee when next Mohammed had a day off work. Mohammed was off on Monday and said so. To get out of their tiny apartment and speak with someone his age in his native language sounded appealing. They set a time and a meeting place. Mohammed didn't see him again until Monday.

The man, named Amar, asked Mohammed many questions over coffee: what he remembered of Syria, why he left, how he felt about living in London, what work his parents had done. At that last question Mohammed went silent. He would not discuss his parents. He said it was time for him go. Amar apologized for being too personal. He paid for their coffees and suggested they meet again the following Monday. "Bring your brother along, too, if he is not working."

When Mohammed told Damir about the coffee, Damir, teased him about his reluctance to talk about their parents. "Father was a respected businessman before the war. People could come to him for help, and he gave it even when they had nothing left to pay him," Damir reminded him. "We have no reason to feel shame about our parents." That ended their conversation.

When next they met for coffee, Amar asked Mohammed a startling question. "Are you from Homs?"

Mohammed could not lie. He nodded, his eyes on the coffee swirling in the cup he had raised halfway to his lips when Amar asked the question. A tremor began in his hand causing the coffee to slide over the mouth of the cup and drip onto the table. He felt Amar watching him, noting his response. Did it never go away, the trauma of war?

Amar apologized for upsetting him.

"How did you know?" Mohammed asked.

"I have known others from Homs. Like you they don't talk about it. You didn't want to talk about your parents. I made a guess." His voice was respectful and kind. And he did not push the river of conversation, which made Mohammed feel he could trust him.

On their sixth coffee Amar said he had something serious to discuss with Mohammed. He said that asylum seekers were being detained at camps across the UK under conditions more like prison.

Mohammed was unclear what this had to do with him.

Amar said that most of them are Muslims. "They are holding our people like slaves, man. Making them work for no pay, separating families. Fuck, man, it is fucking terrible. And we need to do something to help them. Do you agree?"

Mohammed nodded, uncertain.

"This is not why we came here. We came here for freedom, opportunity, to escape the violence of the wars in our home countries. Yet they are putting us in prisons, no rights, caging families behind concrete walls. They talk about the clash of civilizations, about a return of the Crusades, but we believe democratic revolution is what is needed. Liberate the prisoners inside the Bastille, destroy the prisons."

Mohammed had begun to sweat. He wiped his face with the paper serviette and glanced about to see if anyone might be hearing their conversation. Only some white businessmen at a booth talking animatedly about football and couple of students acting inappropriately, fondling each other's thighs, leaning in to kiss.

Amar continued, speaking quietly in Arabic. "This dude we know has drones that carry grenades that can be flown to their targets even at night. They could be dropped on the walls of the detention centers. We control where they are detonated. They are precise. We've tested them. We've flown over the camp in Devon at night at 100 meters to avoid detection and dropped lower to photograph the interior. We have mapped the grounds. We know where the barracks are, where the service entrances are, and where the children are housed. We are thinking we can pilot the drones at night to where the walls are closest to the people's barracks. We have calculated where to drop the explosives—a controlled explosion—so that a small section of wall beside an entrance is blown up but not the barracks."

Amar sipped his coffee, attempting to disguise his escalating panic. He looked around the restaurant and then back at Mohammed. "We need people to have cars ready to transport those held in detention. They will come out of their barracks when they hear the explosion. We have other drones that will follow those carrying grenades. They will broadcast directions in Arabic. Of course, some will be too timid to risk it. But others will come out. We will liberate at least some of them before the managers of the camp can mobilize enough security guards to keep them contained inside the barracks. We are looking for drivers to help those we rescue get to safety. Once we have enough drivers, we will deploy them near one of the camps and at the right time begin the rescue. That is as much as I can tell you now."

"This sounds very dangerous."

"It is. But we did not suffer so to get here to allow our families to be broken and violated in British camps. We will be careful not to injure anyone. I assure you, it is very well planned. I am asking you because of what you have suffered. I know you will be sympathetic to our plan. We are asking you to be a driver." Amar scrutinized Mohammed's face, assessing whether to say more. He decided to risk it.

"If you agree, we will send you with a rented ten passenger van to Barnstable to stay for two days. You will make your way around the countryside and familiarize yourself with the roads.

You will be given a phone programed with GPS directions for where to be and which roads to take to get your cargo to safety. We will notify you what day and time to be at your assigned location and where to drive your 'cargo' to safety. After you finish you will return to London and leave the van where we tell you. We will have signed doctors' statements that you have been ill to take to your employer. Food and water will be in the van for you. I need to know if I can trust you. Are you in? I believe your father would urge you to do this."

"I never told you anything about my father."

"We have researched you. We know about him and about your sister who has written articles about the treatment of asylum seekers. Your brother is too young. You will find an excuse to give him for being gone. I will be in contact with you two days ahead so you can tell your boss you are sick. Will you join us?"

CHAPTER 22

On the Wednesday of the hearing Jennifer dressed carefully and conservatively. She wore sleeves long enough to cover the tattoos that ran up her arms in dramatic tones of blue and black. She put on leggings and a skirt, the only one she owned, left from when she sang in a choir and was required to wear black skirts and white blouses for performances. She even made up her face and curled her hair. This was a performance, too. Then she took the Tube to Westminster, arriving just in time for the special hearing.

Because the hearing was closed to the public, they told her to sit outside until called in to testify. She opened her phone and clicked on *The Guardian*. The lead story was about an overnight fire in a set of flats in Essex populated with immigrant families. Casualties were high and at least twenty had been killed. Police speculated that it was caused by arson but had no suspects. The owner of the building dodged questions about whether his maintenance had been faulty and insisted "these people" start fires to cook "like they do in their home countries. You have no idea what I put up with," he complained to the press.

The address of the fire was familiar. When she looked it up on Mapquest, she saw that it was near where Ana and her brothers had lived three years ago, "an immigrant ghetto," Ana had called it. "The only places that will rent to us charge exorbitant rates and subdivide the spaces to squeeze more of us in. It's appalling but most people have no options. They'll not even show them flats in safer, better maintained areas." She remembered Ana saying that the owner of the flat she had rented with her brothers placed a surcharge on the rent to cover damage "you people" do when you are drunk. When she reminded him that they were practicing Muslims and that Muslims do not drink alcohol, but it mattered nothing to him.

The story of the fire reminded Jennifer of the fire at Grenville Towers the year she and Ana met. Grenville Towers was a highrise apartment complex and the fire had killed 72 people, most all of them immigrants.

She had learned so much from Ana. Much of what she'd learned she should have known was part of the world in which she lived. When she said this, Ana patted her hand and replied, without judgment, that Jennifer should not blame herself for her lack of awareness. "It's part of your DNA. The color of your skin and the way you speak English protect you from knowing. You don't experience what people with different coloring and accents experience."

With Ana she had become acutely aware, but she had to admit that she still sometimes overlooked the rebuffs, the cruel jokes, the unintentional patronizing treatment that Ana experienced. Ana, being Ana, looked for the positive, the old man who owned the local grocery who now greeted her warmly and the children who spoke with her out of curiosity, not prejudice asking, "Why do you cover your hair? Why do you wear long sleeves when it's warm outside?" Ana could tell when a question was malicious or even critical. These were the natural questions of children trying to understand their world.

Last night Jennifer had fallen asleep well after two and slept fitfully. These months since Ana's disappearance her dreams had become more graphic, dramatic, and repetitive. Often she was trying to reach a destination and was undermined by one problem after another—green and spotted snakes, men in black woolen caps wearing bandanas that covered all but their eyes, crowds of people circling her, taunting her, hitting her with hoses and sticks. Occasionally in her dreams a woman appeared who from the back resembled Ana. The woman was always some distance ahead, and Jennifer would run toward her, inevitably breaking a heel or tripping and falling. Before she could reach the woman, she was gone, melting into the horizon. Jennifer would wake up exhausted or weeping or both.

She would try to get back to sleep by retelling to herself the story of their love affair. Like a child's favorite bedtime story, the narrative of the blossoming of their love for one another had a soporific effect on her troubled mind, at least sometimes. When that failed, she would huddle against the headboard, body curled around the notebook she kept, studying her lists of possible leads to follow. Or she would get up, shower, dress, and straighten the house. Always before she had been the lax one when it came to tidying the house. Now she obsessively tidied and cleaned. At first it was part of her denial, keeping the house the way Ana liked to see it for when she would walk in the door and normalcy would be restored. Now she manically dusted and hoovered just because. Perhaps it tied her to Ana somehow. Perhaps it kept her from self-destructing.

Sitting outside the hearing room she was lost in thought when the heavy mahogany door swung open and a man in a suit with a plastic encased ID hanging from a lanyard around his neck motioned her to come. She stood and for a moment collected her energy. Then she followed him into the room. There were several cameras and a gaggle of reporters in the hearing room, which was small but large enough to have a dais on which the important people, the MPs, sat looking down on the table with three chairs and three microphones where she assumed she was to sit. Behind the table a fifty-something man sat facing the committee.

She saw Dame Edith sitting in the first row of the dais. Dame Edith's face was unusually flushed. She motioned Jennifer to come to her and Jennifer moved to stand below the dais where they could talk. Dame Edith's speech was clipped, and she seemed distracted. "I am very sorry, my dear, but we have just received some important information that requires this committee to continue with the previous witness. We will have to postpone your testimony. My staff will be in touch with you regarding when we can reschedule." Dame Edith gave her a mechanical smile before standing and approaching the other MPs to confer with them.

Jennifer looked around, confused. The man with the dangling plastic ID had morphed into dozens of men and women similarly attired. She sighted her escort looking agitated and motioning her to exit. He opened door for her, and she heard it slide shut behind her with a resounding thud. What could have happened inside that room? Behind her she felt rather than heard the huge door open again. Two young staff persons whisked past her, each hurrying. They separated to pass her and met up again when she was behind them. They were heading down the corridor in tandem, walking rapidly, their plastic IDs bouncing from side to side. Something was obviously happening. What was going on? She followed them, considered accosting them and insisting on information, but backed down. As she passed the offices they turned into and reached the exit, she felt helpless and terribly disappointed. She had come to testify, to raise visibility to Ana's disappearance. Instead she was dismissed. She pushed her arms into her raincoat, wrapped her scarf around her neck two times, pulled on her hat and gloves, and left the building.

CHAPTER 23

The uproar inside the committee room pleased Dame Edith when she'd had some minutes to process the shock. Brits were, she believed, generally mild mannered, respectful people who rarely raised a ruckus. Of course, in the closed chambers of their lives they might rant about this or that injustice, usually small and frequently to do with the mistreatment of dogs or family members. However, in Parliament they were quite capable of getting loud and unruly when displeased. All to the good, she thought. Especially now. They should be upset and the more upset they were, the more likely action would be taken.

The owner of SmartSecurity still sat in the witness chair. He was an American, mid-fifties, gray-haired, and well maintained. He fit the stereotype of owners of billion-dollar businesses—soft hands, tanned face, expensive suit, tie and shirt, Rollex watch, and a lapel pin of the US and UK flags, their poles crossed. These people wore confidence like a uniform. Nothing daunted them. Probably he had not envisioned the particular line of questioning Clare Harris-Ashton had taken.

"I have visited one of the camps your company manages," Clare had begun. "It very much resembles a prison camp with its eight-meter-high concrete security fence and barracks that look like replicas of Auschwitz. But what most disturbs me, sir, are the babies and small children who have gone missing. Can you tell us where they are and why you have removed them from their mothers?"

Mr. SmartSecurity's face reddened for a moment before his confident mien returned. "I think you must be misinformed, Madam. We do not remove babies and small children from their mothers."

"Last week our delegation, all of them present in this chamber, visited the Devon camp and met with a group of women who told us that women who have given birth in the camp have had their infants removed at six weeks and have not seen them again. Recently young children, toddlers, have also disappeared. We demand an explanation. Where are these babies, these small children?"

Silence filled the chamber as every eye stared at the American. The room appeared in sharper focus. There was a hard-edged raw quality to the faces of spectators. A collective sound followed the silence beginning in the back rows. A wordless sound of shock and disbelief snaked its way forward, past the witness table and surrounded the MPs who sat on the dais looking dazed.

Then Mr. SmartSecurity seemed to reassemble himself, pulling at his shirt cuffs and straightening his tie before he spoke. "We have an arrangement with international adoption agencies to place the babies in their care. It has been so successful that we have expanded our contract with them to include toddlers."

"Just what do you mean by placing these children 'in their care'?" Clare's voice cut like nails on a chalkboard.

"The agencies care for the children."

"For how long?"

"Until they can be placed with adoptive parents."

"You are removing children from their parents and adopting them out around the world without their parents' consent?"

"Their parents sign a paper when they enter the facility that says we may place their children in care."

"What languages are used on these papers?"

"English."

"Only English?"

"Yes."

"What languages do the parents speak?"

"Many. Arabic, Erdu, French, Turkish, Kurdish. Many."

"Parents are signing a document only written in English that you use as legal permission to remove their children permanently from them. Would you say that most of these parents understand what they are signing?"

"I could not tell you that, Madam. The corporation's lawyers modified the document to be legally valid in the UK. Most people in the world today learn English in school. Surely you are not suggesting these children are better off living in an asylum camp than in a caring home with parents who can provide for their needs? Surely you are aware that infertility is at epidemic levels in the UK, the USA and in much of Europe? We consider we are providing an important community service through this arrangement."

Another MP began to question the witness. "How many children have you taken from their parents for international adoption?"

"I couldn't tell you that without consulting my staff."

"Then we ask you to gather this information, by age and name and country of origin, and get it to this committee within the week. Is that understood?"

"Yes." The man's veneer was melting under the lights of the television cameras. His right hand fiddled with his wedding ring, turning and turning it around his finger. "Will that be all?"

The MP was clearly irritated with the question. "You may be accustomed to exercising that power within SmartSecurity, but in Parliament we decide when we are finished with you, Sir. Please tell us what else the asylum seekers are relinquishing when they sign this document?"

"Property they bring with them into the UK. The right to counsel. The right to appeal. That's all."

"May I remind you, Sir, that you are paid by His Majesty's Government. You are under the laws of this government. The rights you say that persons seeking asylum lose when they enter your facility are rights guaranteed to all Brits."

"These people are not Brits. They are aliens, foreigners, whose arrival in this country is damaging the nation's security. I take my instructions from the Secretary in charge of Immigration and Refugees. If you have a problem with what we do, you should take it up with her."

That the man was agitated there was no question. He could hardly remain in his seat. His cheeks were dark red and his eyes sparked with irritation.

"The Chair requests you to include in what you provide this committee an itemized spread sheet of what you and SmartSecurity are paid for the ten camps you operate in the UK. Am I understood?"

"Yes, Sir."

Clare received recognition from the committee chair. "I believe this committee needs to meet in closed session after what we have learned today. Does the Chair concur?"

The Chair did and gaveled the session to an end, dismissing Mr. SmartSecurity with a reminder that he must give details on the children and babies removed from their mothers to the committee within the next five days.

CHAPTER 24

The next morning's *The Guardian's* lead story was the seizing of asylum-seekers' babies and toddlers for international adoption.

That afternoon tens of thousands of people demonstrated before Parliament, many women with their small children. They carried handmade signs reading, SHAME! and THESE MIGHT BE YOUR CHILDREN and STOP SELLING BABIES. According to one news outlet, hundreds of others, mostly women, gathered in Devon outside the high wall of the camp the MPs had visited. They came with tents prepared to spend the night despite the cold and used amplifiers to sound messages of encouragement to the people confined, messages in English and in Arabic. The Ultra Prime Minister dispatched His Majesty's troops to break up their informal camp. One headline read, "Another Greenham Common?" referring to the women's peace camps outside an RAF base equipped with nuclear cruise missiles in the 1980s.

In Dame Edith's office the Gang of Four gathered to strategize. Clare reported on their visit to the Devon camp. She described the conditions, the fight they had to put on to get access to the women they had met with, the small piece of toilet tissue passed to her that read BABIES in brownish blood. She reviewed the hearing, especially the testimony from the owner of SmartSecurity, and his shocking revelation that babies and now toddlers of women at the camp were being placed for international adoption. Clare also reported that her committee had been receiving quite hostile Tweets and phone calls since yesterday's hearing, although the large gathering in the streets outside Westminster was encouraging.

Hugh reported on his visit with the Homeland Security deputy and his ability to get only one piece of information—that there are three women held in the camps who might be Ana Amara, identified by facial recognition software. That was as much as Homeland Security would supply, no list of asylum seekers held and no access to the three women.

Donald MacKenzie was quiet as usual. Dame Edith asked whether he had any success with his contacts. No luck with his old MI-6 contact, but at the end of the week he would meet with an Arab professor from the University of Sussex. He would keep them apprised of what he learned.

"What is our plan, friends?" Dame Edith was concerned about how to cultivate public outrage. "Yes, there were tens of thousands in the street today and by weekend if we're lucky, that will multiply. But tomorrow the media will have different "breaking news" stories, perhaps including a tangential story on the epidemic of infertility. There will be five or six women interviewed who will tell how after years of trying to get pregnant and no luck trying to adopt, they had received a baby, thanks to the Immigration and Refugee Services program. Their lives are complete now, and they are most grateful to the government for this program. They will say getting the baby of an asylum seeker was a miracle."

Hugh, watching her, thought what a brilliant woman she was and how glad he was for their friendship.

Clare suggested that her Child Welfare Committee could investigate the agencies receiving the children, how they are treating them, and how Brits and internationals can obtain a child. If there is a fee charged, as there certainly would be, what was it, who received it, and…?

Donald was consulting his phone. He looked up with such a look of dismay that Clare stopped mid-sentence. "The Prime Minister has set a debate in the Commons on this subject for tomorrow. That gives us no time to organize or investigate anything."

It took little imagination to forecast how such a debate would be handled with the Commons controlled by the Ultras. Having this debate so soon after the revelations before the Child Welfare Committee played into the hands of those to whom asylum seekers were the scum of the earth. It would let the issue sizzle for two days and then burn out. When the Gang of Four had more information and requested further investigation, they would be dismissed as over-reacting, bleeding heart liberals. We've already had a full debate on this issue, they would be told.

Donald's news soured the room. The four MPs in Dame Edith's office sat dejected, unable to think of a way to counter this offensive strategy of the ruling party. For once, even Dame Edith was speechless. Eventually, one by one they returned to their offices.

CHAPTER 25

The morning after the rambunctious hearing MPs gathered in clusters in the House of Commons. They resembled a colony of penguins assembled in waddles, backs hunched, heads down leaning toward each other. The air was seeded with distrust and anxiety.

The Speaker of the House of Commons entered the chamber walking rapidly. The very air seemed to part to give this confident, charismatic man access as he strode to the head of the room. One might think he was the most important person in the chamber with his white hair standing perpendicular to his scalp in defiance of convention. He pounded his gavel and his thunderous voice declared "ORDERRRR." He overpowered the conversations taking place across the chamber causing the clusters of MPs to break up in deference and scuttle to their seats.

The Ultra Prime Minister rose and waited for the Speaker to recognize him. That achieved, he launched into the reason for this special session. Some MPs on the other side of the aisle were raising a ruckus in opposition to a policy of the Home Office's Secretary for Immigration and Refugees that permitted international adoption of children brought illegally to the UK and held in detention. He emphasized "illegally." He commended the Secretary for her creative collaboration with British citizens originally from the Middle East. She wisely had assembled an ad hoc group of prominent Brits who had started their successful lives here as refugees from the same countries now hemorrhaging people seeking asylum in the UK. The task of this advisory group was to identify how best to handle the tens of thousands of asylum seekers and their children. "There are 75 million of these aliens world wide! It is quite overpowering and threatens the survival of our hallowed way of life," the Prime Minister stated. "On their advice the honorable Secretary recommended, and the cabinet approved, the policy under scrutiny today."

To a shouted question from the other side, he added that the members of the ad hoc group served under an agreement that their names would not be revealed to the press or the public for fear of reprisals by terrorist groups. He could report that their countries of origin are Syria, Saudi Arabia, Qatar, Egypt, and Nigeria.

This was news to the MPs, who turned to each other to express their surprise setting off a tidal wave of sound that rolled across the chamber until the Speaker pounded his gavel and used his penetrating voice to bring the chamber again to order.

The Gang of Four sat separately on the second and third rows across from the Prime Minister. They had agreed to "seed" the chamber to better monitor side conversations among the opposition and identify potential allies who could be approached to oppose this policy legislatively. Dame Edith was surprised by the amount of dissent expressed as the five hours allotted to this session stretched on. Of course, there were a few MPs even on their side of the aisle who nodded off eventually, feeling the effect of too much alcohol or not enough sleep the previous night. But several dozen stood to be recognized and challenged the policy, and they included half a dozen from the Ultra side of the aisle, she was pleased to note.

The Prime Minister used the argument they had heard from the head of SmartSecurity—this policy is no different than Brits sending their children to the north of England and Scotland during the Blitz to keep them safe. A good parent surrenders their rights in order to protect their children.

The Speaker recognized Donald MacKenzie. Dame Edith noticed that Donald's hand holding his notes trembled, although his face looked quite fierce. "Your argument is specious on several grounds," he began. "Brits using the orphan trains sent their children north as a temporary measure during wartime. They were under bombardment, not housed in barracks behind barbed wire. Their children were housed with families for the duration of the war, not adopted permanently. Also, the Brits gave permission for their children to be taken from them—not the sort of permission your party claims asylum seekers are giving—permission written in a language they cannot read that is not translated for them. A more apt parallel to your policy, sir, would be Nazi concentration camps, if parents there gave their children to the government to legally and permanently 'give' them away to families outside the camps. Such a situation might be understandable and humane knowing what we today know about those camps and their Final Solution. But your government maintains that these camps are comfortable holding centers where the inmates merely experience restriction of movement. If they are so benign, I ask my colleagues what parents would sign away their children?"

A senior leader among the Ultras stood next. He spoke slowly, deliberately, which had the effect of drawing all eyes to him. "The Prime Minister has just informed us that the policy was vetted with British citizens born in the Middle East and is supported by them. That is good enough for me. You Progressives are always touting the importance of involving those effected by policies in designing the solutions. What more can you ask for? I am offended by the suggestion that His Majesty's Government would maintain camps in any way comparable to Nazi concentration camps. Shame on you, sir. You are not a patriot."

Dame Edith winced. Donald was new to the boundaries of discussion in the Commons, unaware of the unwritten rule that one must never even hint that the Ultras shared anything in common with fascists, especially Nazis. She wished he had shortened his argument. By including so many points, he diluted the strength of his argument. Nevertheless, he'd made good points and she was proud of him for speaking.

The debate continued, robust and vigorous. She could see down her aisle that Clare was writing down the names of those who spoke and assigning them to an informal three-columned list: those strongly supportive of the policy, those opposed, and those in the middle who might be moved by more information, a personal conversation, a visit to the camps.

An MP on the Ultra side was recognized. "Certainly my colleagues agree that it is best to rescue these children from the barbarism of their native cultures, give them a chance to become educated and adjusted to Western culture, and rescue them from Islam. I see no reason to be upset by this policy. Think of the girl children it is saving from forced marriages, honor killing, female genital mutilation, and other horrific experiences they would probably be subject to were they to remain with their families."

An Independent MP rose, her brown face frowning so that the red dot between her eyebrows was captured inside her wrinkled brow. "The Member's characterization of Muslim women is a stereotype that does not apply to women in most of the Muslim world. I find it inaccurate and highly offensive and would remind my colleague that his language is offensive to 13% of the population of London, our capital city. I am not Muslim, but I know many Muslims from my country of origin, India, and from other countries. I ask the members not to express spurious and untrue information in this debate."

Her remarks set off a buzz that the Speaker quickly pounded to silence. It was clear that Parliament was bitterly divided. When the allotted five hours had elapsed and the mood in the chamber had become increasingly hostile, the Speaker ended the special session.

The Four gathered in Dame Edith's office after the session ended. They agreed that the ad hoc group recommending the policy had been the most damaging talking point of the Ultras.

Donald asked if there was any way they could learn the names of those involved—or the size of their contributions to the Ultra Party. Surely the media would be willing to expose this information if it showed, as he expected it would, a link between major donors to the Ultras and the members of the advisory group.

"Perhaps it is time to mine our own contacts among the migrant communities from those countries. They are probably aware of who among their group support the Ultras, don't you think?" Donald suggested.

"But who do we know in these communities? For all we say we support diversity in Britain, my own social circle is virtually all white, I must confess." Sir Hugh looked at each of them in turn, his face showing he hoped he was wrong, but no one disagreed with his observation.

"I could get in touch with Professor Fayed, although I detest his politics. Perhaps if I am very intentional, I can play up to him and get him to brag about the Saudi billionaires he knows." Donald was beginning to catch on, Dame Edith observed to herself. She nodded encouragingly in support of his suggestion.

Clare was reviewing the notes she'd made in her tablet during the debate. "There were sixteen women MPs who expressed concern about this policy. Perhaps Dame Edith and I could visit with each of them in the next week to try to fuel their concerns and recruit them to join us."

Dame Edith kept to herself that even if all of them were persuaded, that amounted to only twenty out of six hundred and fifty MPs. Instead she proposed they invite all sixteen to a coffee tomorrow with the goal of getting them to visit the camps in weekly delegations for the next month, extending their visits to camps other than the one in Devon. Recruit them to be truth seekers and to focus on the women's barracks. Each one who returned from a visit appalled would become an expert witness and would pledge to talking with other colleagues and the media about what they learned. This strategy would allow their circle of opponents to the policy would grow.

"All right. We have a plan." Hugh had another appointment and needed to leave. "I will get back to my contact in MI-6 and see what more I can learn from him."

The small band of crusaders began to disperse. No one named the obvious: that the day's special session had diminished their already insufficient capacity for challenging the party in power. Dame Edith turned on the BBC as Hugh was heading out the door. On the screen a pretty young woman was announcing "breaking news."

"Norway and Turkey have just passed resolutions calling for an investigation of Britain's treatment of people seeking asylum. They acted on the principle of Universal Jurisdiction, a principle accepted in international law since 1998. The governments of both nations have brought court cases to their nations' courts charging the UK with criminal violations of international law by permanently separating children from their families. Their actions came following media reports that the minor children people seeking asylum in Britain are being taken from them and adopted by nongovernmental organizations in other nations. Norway and Turkey are bringing resolutions to the UN where both are members of the Security Council.

Clare rushed after Hugh, calling him to come back to the office immediately. They stood together listening to the news report, watching the screen shift from maps highlighting Norway and Turkey to drone photos of one of the camps and pictures of the day's debate in the Commons.

Dame Edith spoke. "At my age I should know that anything can happen. My Irish grandmother used to say, It is always darkest before the dawn."

CHAPTER 26

Only one person knew where she was. Before she'd been kidnapped and delivered to the camp, the two of them had talked about masterminding a break-in of the camp that might release even a few prisoners to get the word out about how asylum seekers were treated. She hadn't planned on actually living in a camp, but she had accepted the fake ID he had offered her, just in case she needed it. She used it here and by some fluke they accepted it as accurate. Her career in journalism had made a sudden turn--working undercover in the Devon camp. Muslim women were invisible in this environment, cloaked in the uniform burqa and hijab. The invisibility enabled her to investigate and collect information, to be an acute observer. Memory replaced technological ways to record what she learned. She taught her brain to use individual names as files that she filled with the stories of inmates in her barrack and what they experienced here. It was like learning a new language. Of course, it was lonely, but this mental work helped distract her from the pain she felt when she thought of Jennifer, Mohammed and Damir and the fear that she might never see them again.

One bright autumn morning as she sat at her work station, a woman working across the room suddenly passed out, her head hitting the table with a crack. The guard who had stood behind Ana, raced to the woman who had fainted, not noticing that he had dropped his latest digital toy as he ran. The buzz of concerned conversation among the usually silent women workers further distracted the guards. No one saw Ana retrieve the tiny square camera, snap photos of the warehouse and the guards, and slide the camera into a hole she picked in the hem of her burqa. It was a lucky break.

That evening she lay on her cot in Barrack #24 and gazed at the late afternoon light that illuminated the open portion of the barred and shuttered window above her. She could see luminous shades-of-gray cloud stacked on top of each other and lit from below by the setting sun. She rose and went to the window. Such were the small pleasures of the incarcerated life.

Suddenly a white van moved into her view and stopped. She extracted the camera from the hem of her burqa and let it take a burst of shots as six passengers exited the van and hurried into their barrack. Two of the men were limping, two others covered their mouths with the inside of their elbows. She could hear their ragged coughing. They were all quite thin. She zoomed in on them to capture their faces, continuing to film until the sound of the matron's key in the lock alerted her and she slipped the tiny camera back into its hiding place in her hem.

CHAPTER 27

Donald MacKenzie's meeting with the Arab chemistry professor from Sussex University had to be postponed twice due to the crisis precipitated by the revelations at the hearing and the decision by the Prime Minister to hold a full debate in Parliament on the issue of adopting out the young children of asylum seekers. They finally met over lunch on the Friday after the Commons debate.

Donald entered the restaurant preoccupied and discouraged. He had hoped for more public outrage. Instead, some of his colleagues belabored what they claimed was a parallel situation—the sending of British children to the north of England and to Scotland to escape the Blitz, what they referred to as "giving their children for adoption so they could have a better life." Of course, hardly anyone was still alive from that time, but before he was born Donald's family had taken in two children who were sent north on the orphan trains. He'd grown up hearing the story remembered at family gatherings. His parents were proud of doing their patriotic duty and even prouder that the two they'd taken in were reunited with their parents after the War and, all these decades later, still remained in contact on birthdays and at Christmas and the New Year. A family joke was that those English children now celebrated Hogmanny as enthusiastically as any Scot.

To think that this was a parallel situation infuriated this usually even-tempered man. Asylum seekers' children were not voluntarily sent away from their families. These adoptions are final. Those children will never see their parents again. And it isn't wartime, for God's sake. No accounting for some people's ignorance. Or was it deliberate blindness? Or because many asylum seekers were Muslims?

Professor Fayed was already seated at table in the rear where there were fewer customers. Donald was surprised to see him sipping a pint of ale. They shook hands, made small talk for a bit, and ordered from the menu before Professor Fayed asked just what it was that interested the Honorable Professor MacKenzie in meeting with him. There was a prolonged pause.

"I admit that I am still asking myself that question. I ran for the Commons because of my distress that Parliament is dragging its feet addressing the climate change crisis, but in my first year at Westminster other concerns have forced me to broaden my outlook, specifically our asylum policy and the treatment of Muslim citizens and non-citizens of the UK When I heard that some Muslim Brits have faced discrimination in the workplace, I decided to look at my own former workplace, academia, and start with my own field of chemical engineering. I wanted to speak with chemical engineers who were born in the Middle East and learn about their experience." He stopped, feeling awkward and naïve, and gave Professor Fayed a glance that communicated "help me out here."

Fayed responded with a careful mix of friendly good humor and dismissal. He insisted that he, for one, had not met discrimination but appreciated the MP's concern for "people like me." Then he launched into what felt a bit like Course 101 on Muslims in Britain.

"I'm sure you are aware that Muslims come in all varieties, all colors and language groups, too. Some are Arabs, some Farsi, some African, some Asian—Indonesia is the largest Muslim nation in the world—and some are European Slavs. Some are sympathetic to ISIS and Boko Haram and some are great supporters of nationalist parties. We have a wide variety of experiences and differ vastly in our political beliefs and practices. Like me, for example. I drink." He grinned and took another swallow of his ale, obviously enjoying the taste.

"Here in the UK some of the largest contributions to the Ultra Party come from Arab billionaires who are British citizens. Safir Kabali, Waled Said, and Fariq Abed have given millions of pounds first to the Tories and now to the Ultras. Muslim billionaires increased their donations dramatically once the UK left the European Union. They're major investors in football clubs, hotels, real estate, petroleum and natural gas, of course, and banking. Perhaps of more interest to you, a number of them have funded whole programs at British and American universities. I believe you are a Cambridge man? You may be interested in checking out how much of your alma mater's budget in the sciences and IT comes from Muslim big donors."

Donald's face showed his surprise. He had read about the growing Saudi influence in the U.S. especially under former President Trump, a businessman whose close ties to billionaire celebrities around the world was common knowledge. But he was unaware of Arab billionaires in Britain playing a major role in politics.

"Of course, most asylum seekers tend not to be from those families," Fayed was laughing as he said this. "In fact, they are the people Arab billionaires are happy to see leaving their countries of origin, particularly true of members of the Saudi royal family. Remember that the powerful families who rule that part of the world are not known for stellar human rights records. How many dissidents did Saudi Arabia execute last year? Fifty? Seventy?"

MacKenzie struggled to summarize what he was hearing. "You're saying that while Muslim asylum seekers are placed in detention camps here and their children placed for international adoption, Muslim billionaires—those who have invested heavily in Britain and even become British citizens—financed the election of Ultra politicians to leadership and continue financing them so they will remain in power? And the Ultra party platform is anti-immigrant?"

"Precisely. You scrub my back and I scrub yours. It is the way the world works, my friend. In this case, 'you take our refuse and we'll help you remain in office.' Anyway, better for the refugees that they have a bed and food in a camp than be shot or disappeared in their home countries, wouldn't you agree?"

"Can you tell me more about the funding of university programs, especially in chemical engineering?"

"I can tell you the grants are copious if you want to do chemical weapons R&D. It's the next Big Thing. Dissident groups can make chemical weapons or even nuclear weapons quite simply with ingredients they can buy online or in shops, all under the radar. They are cheap to make and not complicated to use. Countries with powerful dictators want ways to protect themselves from these weapons, and billionaire businessmen from across the world want to protect their installations from attack by dissidents. They also make money by laundering money invested in these projects by parastatal actors, including the mega gang networks. One man's criminal is another man's Sugar Daddy, you know. For people like us, simple chemists, it is best to accept the funds and not ask too many questions about where the funding originated or what subsidiary motives are behind the donations."

Fayed shifted the conversation to his own current research project. Donald felt like he was wandering through a rabbit warren. He was stunned and preoccupied with what he had just learned. Why hadn't he known about the extensive elite Arab power behind the Ultra Party? He was barely following Fayed's description of his research design. After an hour, his head pounding, he checked his phone and said he had to leave for another appointment.

Driving home he felt for the first time that he understood those Brits who moaned about what was happening to their country. Foreigners buying our elections! When he reached home, he dispatched a terse email to the Gang of Four asking for a meeting ASAP.

CHAPTER 28

Professor Ibrahim's quest for a new position brought up a couple of possible options, both troubling for the same reason. Brightly, a private university housed in a Georgian Mansion in East Devon, Lincolnshire, had an opening in its animal husbandry school. That seemed strange. Richton University was ten minutes from the sea and thirty minutes from Exeter. They sought a chemical engineer to direct a grant they received to do research in animal fertilizer. When he spoke with the contact provided at the bottom of the online ad, he was told the research was on low tech transformation of animal waste into explosives.

His other option was at Porton Downs, the top-secret British government facility that was founded in 1916 after chemical agents were used by Germany in World War I. Porton Downs also is known as the Defence Science and Technology Laboratory. He recognized the name from the day that changed his life, the day he had stood in his office in Damascus and heard the BBC announce that, according to tests run by Britain's prestigious Porton Downs Laboratory, sarin nerve gas was used against Syrian civilians by the Syrian government. He would never forget that day or the name Porton Downs where scientists from Britain's top-secret military research facility had found conclusive evidence that the Bashar al-Assad government—the government for whom he worked—had killed 1,500 or so of its own people with nerve gas chemical weapons!

He had found the position advertisement in the Employment section of a professional journal. The description was vague, just "experienced chemical engineer." Now he looked up Porton Downs online and read in a 2018 article that it received £500 million a year from the government and employed more than 2,000 scientists to research ways to protect troops from chemical and biological weapons. He found another article from several years ago about these Porton Downs scientists' conclusion that biological agents like Ebola could be used as a biological weapon of mass destruction.

Surely these chemical engineers were doing important work. But could he trust that they were not designing weapons of mass destruction in addition to researching ways to counter their effects? He had been betrayed by President Assad into thinking his own research was protecting the Syrian people from chemical weapons. But the dictator himself was ordering the use of these weapons on his own people, and only the military would be protected.

After his experience in Syria he had sworn he would never again do research that could be used to destroy the lives of civilians.

He stewed over whether he should at least inquire about the position. He talked it over with his wife Amra and, with her encouragement, decided to seek more information. He made a cold call to the number in the ad and left his name and number in a voicemail message. To his surprise, he received a call back from the director of the program within an hour.

The man sounded quite cordial over the phone and was eager to meet with Ibrahim. With some reluctance Ibrahim agreed to come to Porton Downs for an interview at the end of the week.

The drive to the laboratory took him through a broad expanse of uninhabited countryside, alive with color on this autumn day. It surprised him how rural this part of England was.

They met in the long white single-story building that had been built more than a hundred years ago to house the program. The director, who had sounded so cordial on the phone, was even more so in person. He was probably in his forties, beginning to bald, and walked with a slight limp, a war injury from Iraq, he was quick to tell Ibrahim. The director surprised him by telling him that this laboratory had developed anthrax during the early Cold War, but that by the late 1970s it had stopped researching new chemical and biological weapons and committed its scientists to only defensive research. That commitment was what had drawn the director to accept the job here four years ago. "As a veteran, I want no part in more killing," he told Ibrahim.

The man said he was aware that Ibrahim had not known that President Assad was engaged in chemical weapons production. That he knew this startled Ibrahim.

He also knew that Ibrahim and his family had been harbored in the British embassy in Damascus for a month and then smuggled out of Syria to London.

"Our government assisted you to escape. We've been watching you, hoping eventually to attract you to our labs," the man told him, apparently anticipating Ibrahim's unasked question. "We guessed you had been so badly betrayed by your government that you might not ever again want to engage in weapons-related research. Which is why when you telephoned, I called back immediately and probably sounded over the top enthusiastic about having you come here."

Ibrahim was stunned by how accurately the man identified his feelings. What came next was also astounding. "We want you to work with us. I promise you that we do only preventive and defensive weapons research. We are prepared to offer you whatever it takes to persuade you to join us. Is five times your current salary sufficient for you and your family? We believe you are the ideal scientist to help us research how to protect people from the new generation of weapons made and used by rogue terrorists and state terrorists like Assad. You are, sir, uniquely equipped for this position."

Ibrahim was surprised by the man's candor and by how fast the conversation moved to this job offer. He called Assad a "state terrorist" rather than "president of Syria." He was assuring him that this facility conducted only defensive and protective weapons research. It sounded too good to be true, but could he trust the veracity of what he was told?

He thanked the man for the offer and said he would need to talk with his wife about it. He would let them know within a week. Before he left the man gave him a tour of the facility and told him more about their work. He said one whole department worked destroying hundred year old chemical weapons left over from World War I. The cannisters had been dropped on Britain and were discovered unexploded on the proving ground that is part of Porton Downs. Destroying them was a complicated process that required almost two days for each cannister. It was a sobering part of their assignment. But, of course, that is not what Ibrahim would be doing.

After the man escorted Ibrahim to his car, they shook hands. "I'll be waiting eagerly for your call," he said.

Ibrahim was sweating profusely despite it being autumn and seasonably cool. He had met someone who knew what he had been through, who valued his skills and training and seemed to share his principles. Those facts did not wipe out his experience in Syria, which made him inordinately suspicious. He was uncomfortable with the way Brits he knew reinforced their statements with "I promise you." Can people truly keep all their promises? Did they intend to? Yet, this man had said he promised that they only did defensive research.

Ibrahim needed to find employment. His job at the university would end in a few months.

Perhaps their family could be happy in rural Britain? It was a beautiful area after all, he observed as he drove through the Devon countryside heading back to London.

CHAPTER 29

Donald MacKenzie struggled to explain to his colleagues why his meeting with Professor Fayed so unnerved him.

"The ascent of the Ultra Party to power in Britain is alarming to all of us because of the policy changes it has brought—a veritable end to our middle class, taxation that privileges the super-rich, refusal to curb the warming of our planet that endangers island nations like us, and severe erosion of civil rights for citizens and non-citizens alike. The Ultras are even funding a return to coal production, in the Twenty-first Century when our own nation is threatened by rising sea levels due to fossil fuels warming the planet! But what I learned from Professor Fayed is that the Ultra Party's success has been financed by billionaire business people from the Middle East, especially from the most authoritarian nations—Saudi Arabia, Syria, the Gulf States.

"We've focused on the treatment of asylum seekers and their children. But this matters not at all to these billionaires who are happy to see their own citizens leave en masse for Europe and be dispatched by the UK government to detention camps. They are happy to let Britain cope with these people who have, in many cases, been the democratic voices advocating for more open political systems in their countries, the 'trouble makers' who governments like Saudi Arabia's are executing. Britain has become their safety valve. Incarcerating them in Britain is a kind of final solution quite harmonious to the goals of these governments. The British people have been played by the Ultras and the Arab autocrats. We've been duped."

At this end to his soliloquy MacKenzie was breathing heavily, his face damp with perspiration. "Honestly, I don't know what to do." He sank into the captain chair Hugh pushed toward him.

Clare pulled up another chair and settled herself beside Donald. She took his hand in hers and didn't say anything. Dame Edith did the same on his other side. Hugh, uncomfortable with the emotion and the silence, moved to the cabinet where he kept his liquor and poured himself a glass of Glenfiddich. He sipped a long draught and then spoke.

"You've named it, Donald. And none of us know what to do. So maybe we just sit for a bit and try to sort it out over a drink. Anyone else for a Scotch?"

Eventually cell phones ringing and aides knocking on Hugh's door interrupted their silence. "No rest for the weary," Dame Edith said standing. Clare was already at the door, but she turned to squeeze out a question, and they each noticed how pale she looked. "Can we meet on this over breakfast tomorrow? Perhaps a night's sleep will provide us insight." Her expression said she doubted it.

Hugh, always the gallant, feigned an upbeat tone: "I'll arrange coffee and croissants here at 8. An incentive to entice colleagues to join us? They don't have to know we are trying to preserve civilization as we have known it."

They smiled bleakly at him and departed in silence.

CHAPTER 30

Aaron Geronsky had been doing his own private research on the camps for asylum seekers. His boss was on leave this week, so Aaron could use his lunch hours to locate what had been written and published on the subject. He discovered that several years ago centers for refugees in Dover, Haslar and Dorset had been closed. The public was told the closures were to reduce the number of people in detention and "improve the welfare of those detained." However, since the electoral victory of the Ultras in 2024, the camps had tripled in size and in numbers of barracks, and measures "for the detainees' security" now included concrete walls topped with razor wire like he'd seen in the camp he had visited.

His research turned up a new provision dated March 2019 that stated that those with access to two million pounds over two years to invest would be welcomed to settle in Britain. Those who were stateless must demonstrate they have tried to obtain a right of residence or nationality in another country before they would be eligible to receive from the British government the right to stay for up to five years. Aaron wondered where people stayed while seeking this alternative nationality or right of residence. And what happened to them after five years.

One name stood out in all the reports from the private companies running the camps and in Home Office reports to Parliament on the current status of immigrants to the UK— Andrew Shale. Shale was the consultant hired by His Majesty's

Government to investigate conditions in the camps and the welfare of "vulnerable persons" held there. His first report had been scathing, so scathing that many of his 2015 recommendations had been adopted by the government. Specifically, the government would add a category of "adults at risk" that would include "victims of sexual violence, individuals with mental health issues, pregnant women, those with learning difficulties, post-traumatic stress disorder and elderly people" who could not be held in detention camps.

Then why did the MPs find pregnant women were held in the barracks of the camp they visited, he wondered. He kept reading.

Three years later Mr. Shale had conducted a follow up study and reported he was gravely concerned at the disconnect between the language of government policy and the actual implementation—or disregard for—that policy on the ground in the camps. He could find nothing more recent from Shale or any other reports from outside investigations from the past three years, although he did find a report to Parliament by the Ultra Prime Minister after the last election stating that the Home Office would conduct its own assessment in 2025.

Aaron searched for contact information for Andrew Shale and found it. He was in Oxford working with a human rights organization. Without waiting to think it through, Aaron dialed Shale's number. A chirpy-voiced young woman picked up and responded to his request to be put through to Shale with, "I'm sorry, sir, but Mr. Shale is on a factfinding trip in Myanmar investigating the situation of the Rohingya refugees there. He should be returning at the end of the week. Would you like me to have him call you?"

"I would like that very much," Aaron replied and gave her his mobile phone number. "Probably best if we talk by phone," he said when she requested his email.

If he was lucky, he would have some answers by next week.

CHAPTER 31

After five days in "the closet" as they called it, Mali returned to Barrack #7. She retained her elegant bearing despite the solitary confinement. She also retained her kindness, although she looked weary and her skin was ashy. She resisted the other women's questions about what she had experienced. They gathered around her after the matron switched off the light and locked them in that night. Each woman reached out to touch her arm, her head, her back. They were trying to welcome her to their temporary "home," and to let her know that they cared about her.

Mali wanted to know what had happened with the delegation of MPs. Had their courage in speaking about the pregnancies been rewarded by any changes in their treatment? One of the women whispered that she had overheard the guards talking about the TV coverage of the visit when she had left her place in the warehouse to go to the toilet. Apparently, Parliament had discussed these camps, but she didn't know more than that.

The pregnant woman was now seven months into her pregnancy, which could no longer be disguised. Mali made her way in the darkness to the cot on which the woman lay. "Are you all right?" she asked.

"Yes. All right. And you? I have worried about you. I've been praying."

Mali sighed communicating exhaustion and more. "I survived," Mali said quietly. "We will survive."

CHAPTER 32

Mohammed drove the white van with Smith Greengrocers painted on its sides west of London, taking the highway and exiting at Swindon to follow the country roads that meandered through Salisbury and Glastonbury and on to the seaside. They had booked him a room in Barnstaple from which he was to practice the route early tomorrow morning while it was still dark.

He wore jeans and a T-shirt with the British flag sprawling across its chest. He'd been told what to wear, where to stay, and even what to order for his meals—fish and chips or steak and chips and porridge for breakfast. He was to look as British as a twenty-something Syrian man could look.

He located the small cell phone under the driver's seat of the van along with its charger. Stacked in the rear of the van were several boxes of nonperishable groceries. The mission would take place tomorrow evening barring unforeseen weather problems, in which case it would be delayed 24 hours. He would purchase fruit and milk tomorrow, once the coded signal came through.

He checked into a small hotel that looked like it had been built in Shakespeare's time and not improved since. He ate a meal of fish and chips and disgusting mashed peas and went up to bed. Best to get a good night's sleep, he thought, but sleep was hard to find with the whirl of anxieties circling his brain.

His phone buzzed at two a.m. "21 of us tonight for fish 'n chips," a thoroughly British voice stated before hanging up. Twenty-one was the time, eleven p.m., well after dark. Mohammed tried to go back to sleep for another couple of hours before making the practice run. When he couldn't, he turned on the telly in the small room and watched several old episodes of "Fixer Upper," the series for people interested in purchasing houses that need considerable work. He and Damir had talked about doing that. They might have been able to do it if Ana had not left them for Jennifer. With three incomes, however small, they might have had the money for the initial investment.

He lay back on the bed and allowed himself to think about Ana. Might he possibly find her tonight at the detention camp? What would he say to her if he did find her? She had shamed their family, the memory of their father and mother.

If he was totally honest, he could not say that. Their father had been a respected business man in Damascus, a progressive member of the Ba'athist party. He was not particularly religious, more of a cultural Muslim. He read Western books, listened to the BBC and read the International Edition of the New York Times once a week. Perhaps Ana preferring women would not have upset his father.

Their father owned a franchise of shops in the Damascus Suk and a candy factory that was Syria's largest supplier of Jordan almonds. Mohammed's mouth watered as he remembered the pink and white sugarcoated almonds displayed in tall barrels at the front of so many shops in the huge, ancient covered market. Father had not been particularly politically active, not under the former president Hafez Assad. He had willingly displayed the president's photo in all of his business facilities. But when the son Bashir replaced his father as president of Syria, their father's views had changed, especially after so many groups formed calling for democracy in Syria.

He moved them to Homs but the war found them there and they were lucky to survive the repeated bombardment that didn't spare hospitals or schools or civilian homes. Father tried to remain non-political, but it was difficult, caught between a number of factions and under the government's artillery fire. They retreated to Damascus where Mother's feeble heart succumbed.

When in 2013 word came that President Bashir Assad had authorized the use of chemical weapons against Syrian civilians in a suburb of Damascus, killing at least 1,500, Father had taken the president's photo off the walls of his factory and his shops. It was an act of assertion that surprised his family. He had shown no other signs of political activism, but shortly thereafter he told his children that they must leave Syria. There was nothing to keep them there with their mother's death, and he feared his growing dissatisfaction with the government might endanger them.

Then, one Saturday evening after dark, armed guards had arrived at their door to take their father away. Mohammed and his brother and sister could do nothing but wait in terror, paralyzed by indecision. Within a week the state television broadcast the executions of "enemies of the government." Jabril Amara, was among them.

Ana had been working as a journalist and receiving accelerating cautions from her boss about what she was writing. After a major confrontation with her publisher, she began packing. She had been withdrawing cash from the bank gradually over the previous months at Father's suggestion. Within twenty-four hours of father's execution, she and her brothers were in a car being driven west across the Bekaah Valley and over the mountains to the border with Lebanon and then on to Beirut. Their driver was a colleague of Ana's from the paper. He joined them in applying for asylum at the British Embassy.

The year between Father's removing President Assad's photographs and their arrival in Great Britain were a blur to Mohammed, a collage of out-of-focus memories with a multilingual, babbling soundtrack. Their years in Britain continued that soundtrack. They went from being affluent to poor, prominent to parasitic, a family closely bound by love and respect to isolated individuals lost in depression and fearful of the future.

And here he was in a guesthouse in Barnstaple hours away from taking an action that could land him in prison or worse. Britain had reinstated the death penalty in the previous year.

His life had fractured into pieces that seemed unlikely to be reassembled into anything coherent. Was this what had happened to his father—political actions by those in power precipitating an avalanche of doubt about a government he had passively benefited from? Being carried away from his comfortable life to a public hanging after eight hours of torture?

In Britain Ana had told him what she was reading about Assad's imprisonment and torture of tens of thousands of Syrian dissidents. Her findings were central to Human Rights Watch's report on Syria that said President Assad had used chemical weapons at least fifty times on his citizens.

Mohammed knew that his sister was stronger than he was. His way of coping was to shut off memory and mention of what was happening—ban all remembrance of Homs, of the tortures and executions, of what had happened to their father and so many others. He limited his world to the Mediterranean Restaurant that employed him and the rare conversations he and Damir had with other Arab speakers they met by chance. That had been true until he met Amar, whose arguments had drawn him into playing a role in the attempt to liberate the asylum seekers from detention camps.

In a way he felt his own kind of liberation at having something concrete and clear to do about the chaos that had descended on his family and on so many families. Tonight his courage would be tested. He would play his own small part in resisting the evil that seemed to expand from the world he grew up in to the world he had fled to. Maybe swinging from a noose would be better than this half-life of fear and phantoms

Two hours later he was on the road practicing the route he was assigned. The vibrations of his mobile phone, his personal phone, surprised him. It was Damir. "Are you OK?" his baby brother asked. I called your work and he said you were home sick."

"I'm fine," Mohammed answered. "I needed a break and went to the countryside. I should be home tomorrow. If I'm not back, I want you to go to Jennifer, see if you can move back with her. Will you promise me you will do that?" He was trying to take care of Damir without giving him any information that could incriminate him.

"You sound weird." Damir sounded worried. "Seriously, are you really OK? I didn't think you'd ever make up with Jennifer."

"I'm fine," he repeated, "and I'll see you tomorrow night. If I'm late you…"

"Go to Jennifer."

"Right. Ciao." He clicked off.

Mohammed's phone said it was 6:30 when he returned to the hotel room. He would sleep till late afternoon and then purchase the groceries, have a meal, and start out. He checked the phone they'd left for him in the van. A one-word text had come in: "On."

As dark engulfed the countryside Mohammed drove along the rural road their GPS directed him to. He was approaching a quiet wooded area and slowed, looking for the wall that should be on his right. He almost missed it. It wasn't marked on the directions they'd supplied him and was nearly obscured by the clouded, starless sky. He pulled over. He was to wait until a bright flash signaled that they had breached the wall and opened the gate. They had told him little, only that within five minutes of the flash people would begin coming through the wall to his and the other six vans that were parked under the trees. A drone would light the way. Once his van was full, he was to drive to the sleepy village of Burton on Seaside to deposit his passengers and the boxes of groceries at a boarded up former church. Someone would be there to meet them. Then he was to drive the five hours it would take him to get back to the Tower Hill area of London, leave the van where he'd picked it up and wipe down the dash, steering wheel, and door panels to remove fingerprints, and go home. Of course, if he was pursued, he was to follow Plan B.

He waited.

CHAPTER 33

The women locked into Barrack #7 relaxed on their cots, glad to be free of their burqas on this unusually warm October night. They conversed quietly waiting for sleep, their nightly routine. Mali was the only woman standing. As usual she made the rounds checking on the women who seemed depressed or debilitated. Her last stop was the pregnant woman on the bed beside Mali's, who was already asleep.

A sudden flash of bright light ruptured the dark. Several women stumbled to the shuttered windows to peer through the narrow rectangle where the shutters had been left partly open for ventilation. "Something is happening outside," one whispered. A soft "POP" sounded at the front door of the barrack and they heard the door wheeze as someone pulled it open. Then a voice, authoritative but not belonging to the matron, told them, "Come now!"

Some of the women did not hesitate. They pulled on their uniform burqas and followed the voice to the dimly lit outdoors where a drone hovered overhead. A beamed LED light focused on the service entrance to the camp which stood OPEN.

They fluttered through the doorway, and, lifting their burqas to enable them to run, raced for the open gates. They resembled a flock of gigantic black birds.

Some of the women hesitated, looking this way and that trying to locate the barrack that housed their children. A male voice with an Arabic accent called them on. "We have only a few minutes to get you out. Come now. There is not room for everyone." Most of the women from Barrack #7 stumbled after the voice but a few sank to the ground, confused and full of indecision.

Mali stood in the doorway to Barrack #7, her arm supporting the pregnant woman, urging her forward. But the woman resisted. "I cannot go. I cannot. I am safer here. If they see me this way, they will kill me." She pushed Mali away from her. "You go." She returned to her cot clinging to her burqa like a child to her comfort blanket. Mali finally let her go and fled toward the service entrance.

CHAPTER 34

After the matron had locked them in that night Ana had questioned a couple of women in her barrack about their experiences, where they were from, why they sought asylum, and what had happened to their children. She committed their stories to memory like she had the others she had heard during her months here. She made up raps about each person and practiced their stories inside her head like the spoken word poets she and Jennifer had heard perform. She had no other way to record them. This night two women told her they had heard rumors of young men filling the infirmary, men with hacking coughs and rashes who could barely walk. Were these the young men she had photographed several days earlier?

When the service entrance gate blew open and a bright light shone from a low-flying drone lighting a path between the barracks and the service entrance, the women in Barrack #24 startled and cried out. What was happening? They rushed to the door that exited on the common area, but it remained immovable. Outside they could hear what sounded like a great wind rushing past. They could see nothing through the locked and bolted door nor through the windows whose shutters left only a forty-five-degree angle view of the outside.

Ana assumed this was the break-in she and her contact had hoped to bring off. But how could she escape the locked barrack? She thought she saw dark forms flowing past the sliver left by the almost-joined shutters toward the service entrance. She ran to the opposite side of the barrack. More black forms were moving in the same direction. How had they escaped their barrack? The women in Barrack #24 whispered to each other trying to make sense of the activity outside. Some of them pounded on the door with the spartan furniture in the room. One woman who was especially tiny stood on a bed she'd pulled next to the window reaching her arm outside, waving and calling out: "Here! Let us out! Here!" Her action gave Ana an idea. Standing by the opposite window she called, "Please, take this with you." She rested the tiny camera on her palm, but none of the scurrying shapes stopped. She could not blame them.

Mali saw a haze of dust where the service road ran away from the camp. The exhaust of the vans that were speeding away hung in the night air, illuminated by the drone. She heard the engine of the last van start up and she ran toward it, waving her arms and calling, "Wait." The seventh and final van pulled up to her with its side door slid open. Eager hands reached out to haul her inside. Then it accelerated, leaving a stream of white smoke behind as it raced down the road and out of sight.

The whole operation was accomplished in less than fifteen minutes.

After a very short time, alarm sirens began blasting so loud that Ana pressed her hands over her ears. She could hear voices shouting, men's and women's, a cacophony of noise indecipherable and overwhelming.

The black forms no longer flitted past her sliver of the outside world. The light of the drone was replaced by stadium surveillance lights, glaring sulphurous and yellow. If she stood against the right side of the window, she could almost make out the service entrance where uniformed men now swarmed with flashlights and military weapons. She could see blinking red lights and green heat-seeking tracks. The camp operators appeared flummoxed by the break-in. Now the matrons in a group marched across her sliver-view, some still wearing their pyjamas. It was comical to see the disorder and upheaval here where nothing was ever permitted to be out of its assigned place. She smiled despite her disappointment. "They can take everything away from you except the most precious of human freedoms," she remembered reading in a book by a Holocaust survivor, "the ability to choose your attitude in any circumstance."

Their matron unlocked the door and everyone quieted. Her face stern she made her usual bed-count.

"Can you tell us what has happened?" Ana tried to find the right mix of obsequiousness and assertion.

"A terrorist attack," the matron answered. "You are lucky you weren't taken. Those women will be trafficked, sold into slavery, no doubt about that."

Ana lay on her cot attempting to use the strategies Jennifer had helped her learn to cope with her disappointment. Her chance of escape was nil now, a voice inside her head said. She chose to listen to another voice that recalled her favorite childhood place, the swing in her grandmother's garden. Like the other women she was weeping. She raised her eyes to the window. One star was visible through the cloud cover. Then a guard slammed the shutters shut cutting off her connection with the world outside.

CHAPTER 35

It was still light when Jennifer walked through her front garden the next day coming wearily home from work. A figure sat on the step in front of her doorway, a young man curled in on himself, head resting on his bent knees. Her momentary alarm dissipated when he looked up at her. It was Damir! She greeted him, unlocked the door and ushered him inside. But why was he here?

"You've heard?" he asked.

"Yes," she answered. "Let's go to the back garden for tea." She put on the kettle and both refrained from speaking until they were outside again, settled on her wrought iron chairs sipping tea.

It was all over the news. A break in at the detention camp in Devon. Fifty-five people escaped, most of them women. An operation that had all the markings of a sophisticated terror network, newscasters reported, although no one had yet claimed responsibility.

"He didn't come home last night. Told me to come to you if he didn't arrive. I know nothing more."

Jennifer was uncertain what was most surprising: the fact that Ana's brother Mohammed had gone off or the fact that he sent Damir to her. "I'm glad you're here and I'm glad you're safe," she told him. "Ana?" She left her question hanging and Damir answered with a shake of his head.

"Maybe we will hear something now," she whispered. "Of course, you should stay here. I'll just put sheets on the bed and get us something more substantial to eat." She went back into the house and began preparing a simple meal. Damir walked around to the front to retrieve the luggage he had hidden in the shrubbery. Then he followed Jennifer into the house.

CHAPTER 36

Mohammed could smell the cargo of fear he carried. From the rear view window he couldn't tell how many people had squeezed into his van. Had some been left behind? It had all happened so fast he hadn't noticed. He thought the people he carried were all women wearing burqas and hijabs. When he passed a streetlight, he could see two or three of their mouths moving silently. They must be praying.

Well, he was praying, too, fervently, maybe for the first time in his life. His father, a good Ba'athists, was not particularly religious. Did father become so in those hours of torture, in the moment of execution? He shook his head to banish such speculation. Focus! You must get these people to safety.

His forefinger traced the route on the GPS and he swerved to not miss the first turn. From there the route took him on country roads, one after another, to elude possible pursuit, he assumed. In forty-five minutes they were at the seaside. He could see in the distance a solitary building with a steeple on a promontory overlooking the sea. Forcing himself to drive within the speed limit he guided the van along the winding Seafield Road and out onto the promontory. Turning at the small parking lot, he brought the van to a stop in front of the side door of what used to be a church, repurposed now as a museum. For this moment it was again a sanctuary. He got out and opened the van's sliding side door. In the moonless dark no one would notice the burqa-covered women hastening toward the door. "Come with me," he said, and they followed him obediently, asking no questions. He wondered if he would be so passive? Was that what living in an asylum camp did to you? He assumed because they wore burqas they were conservative Muslims. As they passed in front of him, he was surprised by their faces, some Asian, some Middle Eastern, some African, some European. None of the women spoke.

Someone inside the building held open the door and directed the women into a room they could barely see down a hallway. Only one dim light glowed faintly in the interior, but he thought he saw rows of canvas and aluminum stackable cots that another person was unstacking and passing out.

Mohammed hurried back to the van and carried in the boxes of food. He heard a whispered As-Salaam Alekum from a tall brown-skinned woman. Then he jumped back into the van and took off, resisting the urge to speed. He must not attract attention. Fifteen minutes away from the seaside he heard the first sirens. He accelerated. It was important he not be picked up near this town.

Whoever was the mastermind of this rescue operation seemed to have thought of everything. Up ahead was an entrance to the M-5 toward Bristol and he took it. He was breathing more easily now that he could travel at higher speeds. He exited onto the M-4 west toward Cardiff, crossing the bridge into Wales and, at Swansea Bay, turned right following a sign for the Brecon Beacons National Park. He had no idea where he was. He was simply following the "in case you are pursued…" directions, looking for the town of Merthyr Tydfil. There were virtually no street lights in the area, which was good. He saw a sign that read Merthyr Tydfil, 2 KM and turned onto that road, which was one lane and unpaved. He eased the car off the road and under a large oak tree, turned off the engine, and let his body untense for a few moments. Under the driver's seat he retrieved the box of hair dye and two liters of water and set about altering the color of his hair. He doubted it would look blond no matter how long he left in the dye, but he would not look as stereotypically Arab with lighter hair. He swigged some water and relieved himself while the dye set. When thirty minutes had passed, he used one of the liters to work the dye into suds and rinsed it out of his hair. They had even included a small towel under the seat. With this he rubbed his hair nearly dry.

The van was at least a decade old and abundant with dings and dents. Unfortunately, it was white and he worried that the faint light of rising stars would set it to glowing. Were all seven vans white? He hoped not but had not noticed. He debated whether to leave the van here and set out on foot, but decided after deliberation that in the end a young man walking without a backpack on the edge of the national park late at night would attract more attention. He climbed back into the van and started the engine. Ahead he saw an older man walking a dog. He waved and nodded instinctively—before the war people in small towns back home greeted even those they didn't know. He couldn't see the man's face, which increased his unease, but he continued toward the town of Merthyl Tydfil, parking on the outskirts in a secluded spot under a copse. There he dozed until dawn.

CHAPTER 37

Aaron Geronsky met Andrew Shale at Victoria Station. Shale was a bespectacled little man who seemed to wear a perpetual frown. He said he was agitated by the morning news and appeared preoccupied. His attention came into focus as Aaron, over coffee and blueberry scones, acquainted him with why he had wanted to meet. Of course, the past twelve hours had altered everything.

It was all over the news that a group of Muslim terrorists had broken into one of the detention centers, the camp in Devon that Aaron had visited. The Prime Minister had ordered all police and security forces to hunt for the perpetrators of this major breach of national security. The police refused to say much, just that there had been a break-in to the camp and some "residents" had gotten out. They didn't use the word "escaped." No one had been killed or injured and no organization had claimed responsibility.

"Let me get right to the point as I know you will be much in demand today by the media," Aaron said. "When I visited that same camp two months ago, a woman slipped a note into my shoe that read "HELP" written in blood on a scrap of toilet tissue. Then the hearing, revealing that pregnant women are being held, then the testimony by the CEO of SmartSecurity that children of detainees are placed for international adoption, then Parliament's debate on that issue, and now this break in. What do you make of it all?"

"Tell me first why you are so interested?" Shale looked guarded.

"My interest began with the tripling of the budget for the asylum camps and my visit to the Devon camp. I spoke with Dame Edith and the information I gave her resulted in her visit to the camp, although that is not public information."

"I saw that you worked in the Home Office."

"Yes, and my boss has cautioned me not to look into this. It is an Ultra priority, this approach to asylum seekers, he says."

Andrew Shale averted his eyes. He spoke into his pint of ale. "I don't have much time today. Amnesty wants me to visit the camp in Devon and I must leave in a few minutes. I'll see what I can find out. We both know this is an unprecedented time when even basic questions are not only unwelcome but, I fear, prosecutable. It's good to meet you Mr. Gershon. We can touch base next week." He arose, shook hands, and walked quickly from the pub.

Why was he so uncomfortable? The foremost expert on asylum seekers in Britain seemed socially inept to Aaron. How could a person like that elicit confidences from incarcerated asylum seekers or victims of human rights abuses anywhere?

He checked the news throughout the rest of the day, hoping the authorities would reveal more information about the break-in and the welfare of those who had escaped. Nothing.

CHAPTER 38

That afternoon Mohammed, sporting reddish brown hair, arrived back in London. He left the van on the city outskirts after reprogramming its GPS and removing any fingerprints. He had deliberately driven repeatedly over the special mobile phone they had supplied until it was smashed to bits. He threw some of the bits in various trash bins and flushed other bits down toilets in the Tube station. Then he took the Tube to his apartment where he showered, changed clothes and phoned the restaurant to tell his boss he was feeling better and would be in to work tomorrow. When he assured Mr. Apolous that he had a doctor's note, Mr. Apolous' manner shifted from gruff to reserved. "You be here tomorrow for sure," he said sounding truculent.

Mohammed phoned Damir and, when no one picked up, rang Jennifer who was at work, according to her voice message. He left a cryptic message, "Looking for my brother." Then he rang off.

CHAPTER 39

It took four days for the media to discover what had happened to the escaped asylum seekers. The story broke from Cork, Ireland, where a press conference had been convened by a local imam at the Islamic Centre in a suburb of Cork. Virtually every household in the UK was tuned in.

An opaque haze hovered near the ground where the cool concrete of the gathering area outside the Islamic Center met the warm air of yet another autumn heat spell. The imam, wearing a long black robe and a white fez, looked uncomfortable as he stood before a bank of microphones and cameras. Beads of perspiration gathered on his forehead and upper lip, and he swiped them away as he stepped forward. Two others stood behind him, an attractive woman wearing a blue coatdress and a blue print hijab and a short white man wearing glasses that kept sliding down his nose. The imam spoke.

"As-Salaam Alekum. Welcome to the Islamic Center of Cork, Ireland, the religious center for more than eight hundred Muslims in this area of Ireland. We invited you here this morning because we want you to know what we have learned is happening just across the Irish Sea in Britain. The Prophet Mohammed, peace be upon him, teaches us to welcome strangers and be charitable to those in need. That is why we have given sanctuary to fifty-five people who sought asylum in Great Britain and were instead held in detention centers, separated from their families, forced to labor under challenging conditions, and denied basic human rights.

The people of Cork—people from our Muslim community and also from Cork's Christian communities—have come together over the past three days to provide food for these refugees. Mr. Andrew Shale, who has investigated those camps for the previous British government, has interviewed all of those who escaped and will now share with you what he has learned."

Shale stepped to the podium. He cleared his throat twice and pushed up his glasses before he began to speak. "Four days ago one of eleven detention camps in the UK was entered and fifty-five people held there were assisted to escape. The Islamic Center of Cork welcomed them here and cared for them. Representing Amnesty International, I have interviewed all of them. They are all women. The camp is administered by a private company, SmartSecurity, which is the largest of three corporations administering asylum camps in Britain."

Shale consulted his notes before continuing. "In the camps the women, whether religious or not, must wear burqas and hijabs and six days a week must work in a warehouse assembling small electrical parts—work for which they are not paid. They may see their children only during the evening meal when they are locked inside their barracks. Some have had their small children removed from them. Four who I interviewed had not seen their children in months. When they questioned their treatment or the disappearance of their children, two were placed in a small closet—in solitary confinement—for up to a week. Of course, this violates the internationally adopted covenants on the treatment of refugees that have been recognized worldwide since 1951 and ratified by 144 nations, including the UK. Seven years ago the UK Government agreed that pregnant women along with disabled persons and children should not be confined in camps, but two women I interviewed gave birth while confined, and others currently held are pregnant. The UK Government is defying its own policies."

A female reporter shouted a challenge. "Criminals broke into a government installation, damaged property and abducted fifty-five people who were incarcerated. Are you excusing this behavior?"

A male voice joined the challenge. "Harboring people who illegally enter the UK is a crime. What do you say to that?"

The imam moved back to the microphone. "This is the Republic of Ireland, not the UK. Ireland respects international law on the treatment of refugees. The Irish government supports the rights of refugees to decent, humane treatment."

A man shouted from the rear of the gaggle of reporters, and his voice came through like a battering ram. "Why don't you go back to where you came from and take these women with you?"

The woman on the podium approached the microphone. "I am a Muslim born in Dublin, a citizen of Ireland like more 30,000 other Muslims. We come from here." She took a deep breath and continued. "Some of the women from the camp are willing to speak with the press one-on-one within this building and with our volunteers present to protect them. If you wish to participate in an interview, please follow me at the close of this press conference. I believe we are ready to take your questions."

They were pelted with questions. Had the Islamic Center helped organize the break-in to the camp? Where were those who broke into the camp? Would they be harbored here also? How did the fugitive women get here from the UK? How long would they remain here?

Shale and the imam answered each question: No, the Islamic Center was not involved in the break-in. The location and identity of those involved in the break-in was unknown to them. The escaped women came by boat from Wales. They did not know how long the women would remain.

Then Andrew Shale stood silently and waited for the reporters to go quiet. When he spoke, his voice was terse. "I have a question for you. Why are you not asking about the British government's violations of the human rights of these people, many of them fleeing war, their towns and cities bombed, family members killed? Why don't you ask about their welfare? Why don't you want to know about the British government's criminal behavior toward these people?" With that he turned and walked away and the imam closed the press conference.

Within the hour the Irish government issued a statement. "The Irish people well remember their treatment at the hands of the British government for many decades. The government of Ireland will continue to stand for human rights for refugees and asylum seekers. We will not be extraditing the women who escaped from the Devon concentration camp.

CHAPTER 40

After he returned to London, Mohammed Amara had needed to be alone. He went to work and came back to the apartment. Once he entered that private space, he couldn't stop crying. He had no idea why or how to handle the surging despair that came over him for three nights as he lay in bed. What was happening inside him? He had been so angry at Jennifer and Ana, so angry at everything for most of the past three years. Then he had done something to help other asylum seekers, something dangerous, and the fear his action stirred up in him connected him with his father in a strange and inexplicable way. Was that why his tears wouldn't stop? Was he grieving for his father? Was the storm that wracked him when he was alone grief?

He listened with interest to the press conference on the fourth day after the break-in. So they had all gotten safely away…and to Ireland! He felt proud hearing the imam's words. What those Irish Muslims—and Christians—had done seemed brave. They practiced their religion in a wholly different way than the Assads and the Saudi Crown Prince and jihadists who set off explosives in public places.

The night of the press conference in Ireland he returned to the apartment feeling different, like a kaleidoscope had turned and the colored pieces of mirror had shifted into a new design. He called Jennifer and asked if he could come over. His action surprised him. Even more surprising was how good he felt when she said yes.

Jennifer and Damir met him at her front door. She suggested tea in the back garden, and they sat together talking quietly about the revelations of the press conference while music played to cover their words. Damir said Jennifer and he had hoped Ana would be among the women rescued. Mohammed could feel his eyes fill. He felt awkward, uncomfortable, still he said what he was feeling. "I miss her." For several minutes they were silent. He saw Jennifer reach for a tissue and Damir wipe his arm across his forehead as he shifted position in his chair.

"Can I come back?" he asked quietly, not daring to look at her.

"Of course," she said. "We need each other."

That was all. He told them nothing about his role in the break-in, and they didn't ask, though they were watching him intently. When he notified his landlord that they would not renew their lease, when he packed up their few belongings, when he moved back into Jennifer and Ana's house, he felt good, although it was confusing, and the tears, though not as frequent, still visited him.

Two weeks later Andrew Shale would be back on the news.

CHAPTER 41

Ibrahim had taken his family to the Devon countryside at the beginning of the week that saw the break-in at the detention camp. The area was abundant with trees and gardens and rolling pastures. His wife was elated when they found a house they both instinctively wanted to purchase. At the start of the following week he began work at Porton Downs. For now they were living in rented digs. Their belongings would arrive in two weeks.

He had listened to the press conference from Ireland like much of the world and been shocked by its revelations and by the hostility of some in the press to this Muslim community. The Islamic Center was obeying one of the five Pillars of Islam in giving charity and hospitality to the rescued refugees.

His professional prospects having changed dramatically of late, he focused on the job he was beginning and the details he must tend to buying a house and moving. He hadn't felt so happy since before the Syrian war began over a decade ago.

Ibrahim's new office had glass windows along the wall that faced the common office space. He liked how it connected him with his colleagues. His boss's more spacious office was next door. The small ways the man had made sure Ibrahim felt welcome—walking him around to meet everyone, bringing him coffee, taking him to lunch—confirmed Ibrahim's initial judgment that his new boss was kind and would be good to work for.

At the end of Ibrahim's first week on the job his boss came to his office, "just popping by." He closed the door behind him, pulled up a chair and sat facing Ibrahim. His face looked "off" somehow, purple crescents under his eyes and new lines puckering the space between his eyebrows. His words took Ibrahim by surprise.

"I've been given the boot. I'm not to the Ultras' liking, I guess. They just told me a few minutes ago that I'm to be out by five today. I knew I had to see you, tell you, warn you."

"Why would they let you go?"

"They gave no reason."

"What does this mean?"

"I don't know, but I'm afraid they are taking hold of operations here and using them for their own purposes."

"I don't understand."

"Me neither. Just be careful and keep your eyes open. We all sign a nondisclosure agreement to be hired here. They reminded me of that when they sacked me. I'm genuinely sorry to miss working with you, Ibrahim. I'd been looking forward to it. They won't want you to be in touch with me, but in case you need me…" He stood and gave Ibrahim a long, knowing look, only Ibrahim had no idea what he was supposed to know from his look or his words. He slipped Ibrahim a business card on which he'd scribbled his home address and other contact information. He glanced over his shoulder and back, looking awkward and indecisive. Then, without saying anything else, he left Ibrahim's office.

CHAPTER 42

November

Jennifer had heard nothing from Dame Edith since the abortive hearing. Buttressed by her renewed relationship with Damir and Mohammed she decided to contact her to see if anything new had turned up from the women who had escaped the Devon camp.

Torrential rains had settled over England the day Jennifer left work early to take the Tube to Westminster. By the time she arrived at Dame Edith's office she felt like something the cat had dragged in, hair straggly and wet, mascara puddling under her lower lids. The receptionist took a moment to recognize her. "Oh, it's you. You're in luck. She's in. I'll let her know you're here." She passed Jennifer a wad of tissues, presumably to wipe her face, and was back quickly to usher her into the inner office.

"Jennifer, good to see you." Dame Edith was her charismatic, gregarious self. "How about a cuppa on this miserable afternoon?"

"Thank you, yes. I came hoping you'd heard more from the women who were rescued. Maybe one of them knows Ana?"

"Oh, my dear girl, I do wish so, but no one recognized the name or the photograph. It is perplexing to me. We hoped she was among them. But, of course, she might have been moved to another camp. It turns out a pregnant woman did not leave with the others. She told one of the women she was safer in the camp than outside where they could see her pregnant. I wonder what that means."

"It must mean she isn't Ana, I guess, if none of them recognized the photo." Jennifer tried to assemble her face to disguise how devastating this news was. She knew Dame Edith felt badly for her, but at this moment her hold on her emotions was so precarious that the naming of sympathy might undo her. Instead, she changed the subject. "Ana's brothers are back living with me. That helps all of us." She choked on that sentence. Trying to avoid sentiment she had stumbled into it from another direction. She needed to change the subject. She asked, "What are you pursuing now?"

"We are trying to learn who the pregnant woman is and to get her out of there into protective custody. Her baby is due any moment. I will keep in touch with you, Jennifer. Thank you for coming in. I must be off to a meeting." As Jennifer drank her tea alone in the outer office, she had a foreboding that something serious was distracting Dame Edith.

CHAPTER 43

Andrew Shale had not gotten back to Aaron Gershon. He had simply been too busy following up on the information gleaned from his interviews with the women and from an anonymous source who had called him on a secure line and urged him to keep investigating the camps. "Something very serious is going on at the Devon Camp. I can't say more but look at a government facility nearby and follow the dots. It is terribly important, urgent." His caller had clicked off at that point.

Andrew spent a couple of hours immediately after that call researching government facilities near the Devon camp. Military bases? Salisbury Plain with 15,000 troops? The retired RAF bases at Greenham Common and Upper Heyford? Universities with government contracts? Research facilities including Porton Downs chemical and biological weapons laboratories? That was a long shot, except that he had become too disillusioned with the policies of this government to rule out anything. Of course, there were the conspiracy theorists posting about 300 secret military installations in Britain with aerial footage but no names or map references.

He decided he needed to seek help. Working indirectly he contacted Gershon at the Home Office and Hugh in Parliament and through a third party communicated to each what he needed and the urgency of his request for their help. Meanwhile, he debated how to pursue the inquiry he had promised Dame Edith he would make into Ana Amara's whereabouts.

He hadn't told Dame Edith that he knew Ana. Hadn't told any of them looking for her, not the Gang of Four or the MI-5. He had promised Ana he would keep her secret and he took his pledge to her seriously. It was higher priority to track down this illusive government facility and its connection to the camp in Devon.

CHAPTER 44

The night of the break-in when the matron and an armed security escort entered Barrack #7, they had found it empty except for a young woman swollen with pregnancy lying on the floor beside her cot. She was moaning softly and shaking but not, the matron ascertained, about to give birth. She obviously could not be left alone, so they moved her to the infirmary where she could be monitored.

The woman was incoherent. She seemed to be in shock. Her terror had carried her deep inside herself where her life played across her mind's eye. She saw herself as she had been before this nightmare—beautiful, sleek and pampered, coifed and perfectly made up, nails long ovals with embedded gems, hair made shiny with the most exclusive products money could buy. She wore name brand suits and carried matching Gucci bags, never Chinese knock-offs. Inside her home and when she was with other women, she wore the latest fashions. It was only outside her home that she covered in a long black burqa, gloves, and a face cloth that hid everything but her desperate eyes.

She relived the family gathering where by some miracle she had seen her favorite cousin standing alone in the manmade garden. With no one paying attention to them, her misery fell out of her. Because he had preceded her in disillusionment with life within the Saudi royal family, she could talk with him. He was the only one with whom she could be honest. Other family members had cautioned her to be careful around him, he was too openly—dangerously—critical, and the Royal Family functioned as a kind of Mafia. The Godfather films were popular with the Royal Family and many relatives snickered when watching them, but snickering was as far as one dared go.

She told him in those hurried moments that she could not remain here. Despair poured from her eyes and rained down her cheeks. She lifted her face covering just enough for him to see purple and blue bruises beginning in her right eye and spreading over her cheekbones. He saw only a glimpse, surreptitious and partial, but enough to convince him that Hala, the cousin he had always favored, his most intelligent and outspoken cousin, must escape now. They could tell no one. Certainly not her father Jepthah who was head of the Crown Prince's security forces.

Later, in the plane, he told her he had never imagined her marriage would result in this. He ranted about the treatment of women in their country: Do we cover our women so that we don't see them, truly see them, bruises and misery as well as sexuality and beauty? Why do we assume that story book marriages between beautiful people end happily? Why is one surprised that beauty is no guarantee that a husband won't smash his wife in the face, break her nose or cheekbones, won't throw her across the room, batter her with bottles, and burn her with lit cigarettes? Who would have guessed that the Crown Prince, so handsome and debonair and the darling of the Western media, was practiced in brutality.

They had so little time that night unobserved by others in the Family, but once he saw her—really saw her—he said they must take the irrevocable step of leaving. He would fly her to Britain where she could appeal for asylum. They must act immediately.

They left that night with nothing but what they were wearing and the cash and cards they carried. It was a surprise ending to Prince Charming's romance with his lovely Princess. They flew from Jeddah, her cousin piloting his small plane himself while she hovered hidden in the dark, cramped rear of the plane gripping a tarp he'd tossed to her to pull over herself in case someone should approach before he took off.

When they arrived in London, she was no longer a covered Saudi woman, no longer a princess. She was an enemy of the Saudi Royal Family and an "illegal alien" seeking asylum.

Her cousin was shocked when the Brits took her into custody at the airport—she had no passport—and said they were taking her by helicopter to a camp for asylum seekers. By then the deep purple bruises were working their way through the matte makeup she had applied so heavily to them.

Nevertheless, she had never felt such liberation. She was free of her abuser and protected by His Majesty's Government from ever having to be in his presence again. Discarding her burqa she stood tall and proud in her mauve linen suit, her favorite gold earrings and matching necklace. She was free! Being seen with no title to confine her left her breathless. Of course, she was terrified, too, afraid he might be able to find her and force her to return. Her husband was the most powerful man in Saudi Arabia. Her father, as head of his security forces, also was powerful, but, compared with the Crown Prince,... Almost certainly her father, though she knew he loved her, would have to side with his employer over her. Her cousin had vanished into the embrace of his British wife's family who adored him. She was alone.

That first night in the camp admitting office, they told her to remove her clothing and put on the camp uniform, an burqa and a hijab. It was her first chilling moment of awareness that she might not be so free here in the UK. All the women except the matrons wore burqas, they told her. That they did not require the face covering encouraged her, but as the loose folds of the burqa surrounded her, she felt herself disappearing back into the life she had fled.

Before she was taken to Barrack #7 of the Devon Camp, an officer had excused the matron who had been escorting her. He brought her alone into his office. What happened next was unspeakable, shameful, and nearly as brutal as her husband's treatment of her. She had fought him, pushed him away, screamed, clawed at his face, all to no avail. When he forced himself into her, transforming her forever into a dirty, worthless woman good only to be stoned to death, she collapsed, praying for death, her only remaining liberator.

Sometime later that same night the matron had returned to lead her to her bed in the barrack. She could barely walk and averted her eyes from those of the other women, who drew away from her instinctively. Could they smell what had been done to her? Or did they recognize her face from glossy celebrity photos online that paparazzi had taken and been paid handsomely for? One woman, a tall, regal black woman, had helped her into her bed and told her it would be all right. It was how she passed her first hours in first world freedom.

All of the months since then she had inhabited an interior House of Silence and Shame. The thing she discovered growing inside her felt alien and monstrous. It forever marked her and denied her a future. It was taking over her body. She hallucinated wildly. She pictured cutting it out of her and burying it under the garbage or flushing it down the toilet. When she was less frantic, she imagined giving it to someone else and walking away.

The night of the break-in when she had chosen to be left behind alone, everything caved in on her—her fears, her months of isolation, and the departure of Mali and the other women, the women she could not join because of this alien thing inside her. Because of what would be done to her for this violation of her marital vows.

The camp doctor injected her with a medicine to calm her agitation and put her to sleep. For some days they kept her sedated and sleeping. Gradually they reduced the dosage, all the while monitoring her agitation. One night she opened her eyes, fully conscious. She was back in Barrack #7 with a new group of women and the matron was watching her closely.

After the break-in the camp in Devon was under the tightest security protocols. New inmates arrived several times a week to replace those who had fled and Barrack #7 rapidly refilled.

On her first night of full consciousness she saw the officer who had raped her. He was conferring with the matron at the entrance to Barrack #7. It was her first sight of him since that night. She felt nauseous and terribly alone. Yet, in that moment something changed. She determined to take control of herself, her body and her thoughts, to the fullest extent possible for whatever time she had left.

Eventually the man left, and the matron locked the residents into Barrack #7 as she did each night. The pregnant woman lay on her cot facing the wall willing herself to be calm. Like every night the others escaped into sleep, but, unlike any other night, she knew what she had to do. She pulled herself up from the bed and stood, back straight, making no attempt to hide the front of her body. And she spoke. She had not spoken in nearly nine months and her voice was weak and hard to hear when she began. Word followed word. Their sound strengthened her. Her surprising new voice pulled the others back from their dreams.

"I am Hala, the tenth wife of the Crown Prince of Saudi Arabia." She paused, took a deep breath, and continued, louder, stronger, determined to be heard. "I am Hala, the tenth wife of the Crown Prince of Saudi Arabia. I fled my husband's beatings to find freedom in this country, but I could not escape his reach." The women sat up in the dark facing her, listening intently.

"This child I carry is the child of that officer you saw talking to the matron. He raped me my first night here. But it is my child also. I know that my husband will not let me live. I ask each of you to remember me. Please remember me, Hala daughter of Jepthah, and my poor baby. We must tell our stories. Thank you for listening."

She was finished. She lowered her swollen body onto her cot and rolled onto her side. This time she faced the room, the other women whose stories she hoped she would have time to hear. She would not be ashamed, no matter what they did to her. For the first time in a very long time she smiled.

CHAPTER 45

Dame Edith convened a breakfast meeting of the Gang of Four to share what they had learned since the break-in to the Devon camp. She reported that Ana Amara was not among those rescued, nor was she recognized by them. She told them of the pregnant woman who had refused to come with them, who, paralyzed with fear, had told the woman from Mali that she would be killed if she left. Dame Edith felt that they had to locate her and get her out immediately due to her fragile mental state and the rescued women's expressed concern for her survival.

Hugh reported on his conversation with Andrew Shale of Amnesty who had been told something nefarious was going on beyond what they already knew.

Clare reported that child welfare agencies that worked with her committee had brought suit against SmartSecurity resulting in a court injunction against removal of any more children for adoption until the case was heard. "It will buy us a month or more," she said.

Donald MacKenzie said he had met a second time with the arrogant chemical engineer originally from Saudi Arabia, the man who had informed him of the billionaire businessmen from the Gulf States who were bankrolling Britain's Ultra Right Party. Information had spilled out of the man like it was purchasing power. "I guess information shared verbally is the currency of corruption, when people play it like card sharks play high stakes poker. Influencing a Member of Parliament probably appeared to be a big win to him."

The most interesting thing Donald said he'd learned was that a Saudi princess, one of the wives of the celebrity Crown Prince, had left her husband and come to Britain seeking asylum nearly nine months ago. "Apparently, London's Saudi elites have it that she was taken straight from the airport on her arrival to a detention camp. He says the Crown Prince has a Mafia-like operation everywhere, including in our camps, and that the Saudi expatriate elites are speculating on what kind of cat and mouse game he's playing with her. Ironically, her father is head of the Crown Prince's Secret Security. She put him in a rather nasty place, I guess, caught between the Crown Prince and his daughter."

"Did you say she came nine months ago?" Dame Edith had that look on her face, the one she got when she was making new connections and simultaneously commending herself for still being able to do that in her mid-seventies. "It's a long shot, but I wonder if she might be the pregnant woman who was afraid to be rescued for fear she'd be murdered?"

"Could we subpoena the camp physicians for questioning and ask about pregnant women? Even if it's not the same woman, we could gather data on just how many pregnant women are being held. We could start with the Devon camp since it's under close scrutiny, thanks to whomever launched that brilliant rescue." Clare was on a roll, ideas tumbling out of her, and by the nodding heads of the other three, good ideas.

"Nothing on Ana Amara?" Hugh asked.

"Nothing," Dame Edith replied. "But at least we have some important new threads to pull. Sorry, gentlemen, I thought I'd stick in a women's metaphor since we females are continually subjected to your sports ones." She grinned. "Same time and place next week unless anyone comes up with news?"

They were up and out the door. They had settled into a routine that was quite satisfying to each of them, that sense of camaraderie, of being able to accomplish important and compassionate work together. Pleasant to be working with such good people, Dame Edith thought.

By the next morning Clare had had success. The physician at Devon would testify as long as it was a closed door hearing. The hearing was set for Friday, three days away. Dame Edith planned to attend.

CHAPTER 46

Aaron Gershon brought Andrew Shale some potentially useful information when they met on a bench in Hampstead Heath. The major government facility closest to the Devon Camp was Porton Downs. Aaron had never been there but had done some research on the place during his first government job. He'd investigated Porton Downs' secret development of anthrax as a biological weapon during the Cold War. The place supposedly stopped doing any weapons development work two decades ago at least and now focused on developing antidotes to chemical and biological weapons, how to help military and civilian populations survive if they are ever used. Also, he had read that there was a considerable old stockpile of mustard gas cannisters from World War I that Porton Downs was gradually destroying. "Can you believe that? Hundred-year-old cannisters of chemical weapons piled up in the bucolic English countryside. Waiting for the Apocalypse, I suppose."

Andrew was grim. "It's not funny. A stockpile of mustard gas five hours from here? I was in Halabja in 1988 after Iraq used mustard gas against the Kurds. Five thousand people killed that day and as many as 12,000 died later from that attack. You absorb the gas through your skin or eyes or you breathe it in. It can take days or even weeks to die. Outside on your skin and inside throughout your pulmonary system you develop large blisters that are very painful and close off your airway. It's a horrible way to die, and even if you survive, you're likely to lose your eyesight or your voice. Often you don't know you've been exposed. Your nose quickly gets used to the garlic smell and, because it takes time to do its damage, you may think you are out of danger, while you keep taking in more and more of the agent that destroys mucus membranes and other tissue. And if the day is cool, it hides close to the ground and remains effective for weeks.

But how would a stockpile of hundred-year-old mustard gas be connected to an asylum camp? The two men sat in silence pondering. They were getting nowhere fast.

CHAPTER 47

Ibrahim did not call his former boss, although he kept the card with its handwritten contact information in his wallet.

Several weeks later when he needed more information about a specific alkylating agent, he decided to walk over to the building where the chemists whose task it was to destroy the old mustard gas cannisters worked. Before he was within shouting distance of the building, guards wearing camouflage uniforms and toting military weapons were blocking his path and barking questions at him that made him quite uncomfortable. So much for collegiality at Porton Downs, he thought, exiting the area and heading back to his building. As he turned left toward his entrance, he cast a glance behind him and was surprised to see a van unloading a group of men, all of them young, slender and dark haired, in fact, all of them looking Arabic. What could they be doing here? Were they why he had been treated so hostilely by the guards?

All day what he had observed preyed on his mind. He even asked his new boss about the visitors and was told, essentially, that what goes on in other buildings, other labs, should not concern him. That reply deepened his discomfort. When he went home at the end of the day, he told his wife what he had seen. She suggested he tell someone. But who?

At ten o'clock that night he dialed the number his former boss had given him and left his number. That quieted his anxiety enough for him to get to sleep.

The next morning when he opened the door to the driveway where his car was parked, he noticed a folded piece of paper under his windshield. "7 3 Kings" was written on it. Might this be his former boss's peculiar way of communicating? Not being a drinker, it took him a while to decipher the message. Three Kings was a pub half-way between work and his home. Seven must be a time. This James Bond behavior made him uncomfortable and he told his wife where he'd be after work just in case.

At seven the Three Kings was a bustling and noisy place. Ibrahim recognized no one so he took a seat at the bar and ordered a coca cola, much to the bartender's amusement. The man leaned over to him conspiratorially and said, "You'd save some pounds by getting this at the new McDonalds," wink, wink. Ibrahim mustered a smile and tried to look inconspicuous, which, with ninety percent of the customers white males and none of them looking like Arabs, was a challenge.

At five past seven he saw his former boss in the doorway. The man shifted his eyes to signal he preferred to talk outside, and Ibrahim paid for his pricey coke and left. Autumn had arrived with a vengeance, and he wished he'd brought his jacket from his car.

"Let's walk down the roadway a bit," his former boss said and took off without waiting for a response. When Ibrahim caught up with him, they exchanged a few sentences about each of their families and, when the lights of the pub were well behind them, Ibrahim apologized for calling so late and confided his uneasiness about what he had witnessed at work the previous day. The other man was silent. He seemed to be measuring his words, weighing how to respond.

"You were right to call. I was fired because the Ultras decided to remold Porton Downs to serve their interests. I don't know how they've altered the program, but I worry that if you saw young Arab men there, I doubt the Ultras have their best interests in mind. I can pass this information on and keep you out of it."

"You think they're experimenting with chemical/biological weapons again?" Before the words left his mouth he was unaware that this thought had been circling his brain. Now that he'd voiced it, he felt queasy and angry.

"I don't know. If they had kept me on, they know they would have had to fight me to do anything like that. So, it is possibly why they let me go. But I must stress, I don't know. I feel terrible for recruiting you, but I truly thought they would leave us alone. I couldn't imagine them starting up offensive weapon research again. Are you willing to stay on and to watch for any other changes that we can report—that I can report—to my contacts, who would be both unhappy with such a development and have the power to do something to stop it?"

Ibrahim said he thought he could stay, at least until they knew more. The country road had grown quite dark and they turned in step and began walking back to their vehicles. "Thank you," Ibrahim said offering his hand. "I do miss you. You'll let me know if you hear anything?"

"Of course."

"What are you doing now?"

"Consulting with a couple of British chemical companies. But it's only temporary. Too stressful having to bring in contracts… rather like my days playing with a heavy metal band having to get gigs! But I didn't have four kids in those days, two of them in university." He grinned before getting into his Lexus.

CHAPTER 48

The night after Hala named and claimed her identity, Barrack #7 felt different to her. After the matron made her nightly rounds and locked the doors, the difference was evident. That night reminded her of the first act of Tchaikovsky's "The Nutcracker" which she had seen in Riyadh several times. The toys come alive after midnight. It was her favorite scene. The women in Barrack #7 seemed to come alive this night, too.

A middle-aged woman stood and proclaimed, "I am Safir and I left Uzbekistan after my husband and son were detained by the military for running a newspaper that told the truth. I want you to remember me." For a moment Hala thought the woman was mocking her, but the tears on her face were real. She was following Hala.

Marijam from Nigeria introduced herself, and her dark face was no longer a mask but a roadmap of what she had lived through. "My child was stolen from me by Boko Haram. After two years of government promises that they were looking for our girls, I came to Britain with my remaining children so they would not be abducted and they brought us here. I haven't seen my smallest daughter for months. Remember me."

Five women spoke that night. Five more each night after that. Hala had started a lending library where women shared their experiences, painful and traumatic, loaning them to each other. A bulwark against their present trauma. A woman from Syria named Adna said she had read a book by a survivor of the Holocaust who had stated something that kept her going through the bombing of her home, neighborhood, hospital, and school and through the trauma of leaving her homeland to seek asylum. They can take everything from you, but they cannot take away your ability to choose your attitude. "From this moment on my attitude will be solidarity," she asserted and the others applauded her.

That's what we are doing, Hala thought, choosing attitudes of solidarity.

On the sixth night of their new routine Hala went into labor. The older women gathered around her bringing towels and water from the wash room and showing her how to squat to allow gravity to help pull the baby from her. Two of them held her hands, one wiped the sweat from her face, her hair, and one, a doula in her country of origin, told her when to push. One woman who had not seen her toddler sat beside the laboring woman holding her hand and crooning a traditional lullaby from her homeland in a soft, low voice.

Hala was in labor for many hours. In the end a tiny girl child slipped from her womb and was caught by the doula, who tied off the cord and cut it from the placenta with her teeth before placing the baby on Hala's chest. Everything seemed to conspire to bring her baby safely into this island of community in a sea of anonymity and hostility.

CHAPTER 49

The physician testifying before Clare's committee acknowledged that there had been roughly twenty women in the camp who had given birth, most recently just last night. These women are very resourceful, he said.

Clare asked him who the woman was who had just given birth. He was reluctant to answer her question. "We assign them numbers since often we cannot pronounce their names."

"What can you tell us about this particular woman then?" Clare sounded irritated.

"She spent her whole pregnancy with us."

"Did she receive pre-natal care?"

"The basics. Blood pressure checks monthly. They don't like to be unclothed in front of us male doctors."

"Was there anything different about this woman?"

"When she first arrived, yes. She was quite expensively dressed. I remember overhearing the matrons talking about the gold she wore. Then, after the break-in, we discovered she was the only woman in her barrack who had not left. That night she seemed quite distraught. I had to give her a sedative and keep her sedated for several days to calm her down."

Clare and Dame Edith exchanged meaningful looks. "Do you know where she came from?"

"I believe she is from Saudi Arabia."

Someone in the chamber—it may have been Dame Edith—uttered, "Bingo."

"This committee wishes to speak with that young woman, sir. Will you promise us you will make sure she gets here as soon as she is recovered from giving birth?"

The doctor looked very uncomfortable. "I don't think I can make such a promise, Madame."

"Whyever not?"

"Because the woman was removed from my jurisdiction the day after she gave birth. I don't know where she has gone."

"'Has gone' implies she left of her own free will. Surely you mean you don't know where they took her?"

He nodded and Clare gaveled the session to a close.

Two days later *The Guardian* ran a story based on reliable anonymous sources that announced the death of Hala Jepthah, wife to the Crown Prince of Saudi Arabia. Cause of death was an accident suffered soon after childbirth. The article was accompanied by a photo of a beautiful young woman with flowing black hair and laughing eyes looking directly into the camera. Nothing was said about her daughter.

News of Hala's death was read to the women over the speaker system in the warehouse where they were working. Never before had the death of a woman received such public notice. The women in Barrack #7, spread out across the warehouse and deliberately separated from those in their barracks, wept openly. Then one began to chant "Hala, Hala, Hala, Hala." The chant spread table to table, growing organically, stronger and broader as other women joined them. "Ha-la, Ha-la, Ha-la, Ha-la."

Someone shouted from the rear of the warehouse, "We will remember you!" and the chanting continued, ever louder, voices cracking with emotion. No one present would forget that moment.

CHAPTER 50

On the day after *The Guardian* story Donald MacKenzie found a message on his desk, no return address or signature, no information identifying its origin. He phoned Dame Edith. "I've received an anonymous note. I think it might be from Professor Fayed. Only four words: "Saudi Mafia wins again.""

Just then her aide opened the office door and motioned Dame Edith to take the phone. "Can we talk privately?" She recognized the voice. It was the camp doctor.

She had no meetings that afternoon, but the camp was a five-hour-drive from London. "Do you trust a digital conversation?" she asked.

"No. I took today off, pled illness. I'm looking for a parking place, which is impossible at Westminster."

"I will meet you at the kiosk closest to the entrance of the Commons on the Thames side in five minutes. I'll get you a parking space. I should have some perks after all these years."

"I drive a BMW, black."

"That shouldn't be hard to find!" She was laughing picturing the lines of black BMWs hovering around Westminster at any given moment.

She told Donald she would return his call later and walked briskly to the kiosk, arriving as a black BMW pulled up. Recognizing the driver, she got in and showed him to the official parking area for MPs, securing a pass from the attendant whose children she asked about by name regularly. They took the underground walkway back to her office and talked over tea and her stash of biscuits and cheese.

"This camp and probably the others take their direction from the Saudi security forces when it comes to the treatment of Saudi asylum seekers. Definitely in this case. I have treated people who have been roughed up by them. They're barely breathing when they're brought to me. Usually I have to sign the death certificate: Death by accident or suicide. I saw this young woman, this Princess, a number of times, to check her blood pressure during her pregnancy, to sedate her on the night of the break-in, to monitor her while we had her sedated, and to examine her the morning after she gave birth.

"I could tell her pregnancy traumatized her. Judging by the date she arrived at the camp, her pregnancy happened while she was in our custody. I suspect she was raped. The night the women in her barrack escaped she had a mental breakdown. I kept her sedated for several days. Not long afterward she went into labor." His words came out in a rush, and he had to stop to catch his breath.

"Which other camp officials knew her?"

"I've asked the matron for her barrack what she knows, but she's not saying much. Probably planning to sell her story to *The Telegraph*. She did say that the woman told her mates that she didn't expect to live long. Also, she said that Officer Pendleton had her removed from Barrack #7. With her child."

"The baby. Oh, the poor lamb. How can we find the baby?"

"I usually have to check the children they send for adoption to be sure they are healthy, but I never saw this little one."

Neither of them spoke.

"I'm also concerned about some of the men. More than usual are showing symptoms of pulmonary problems, pneumonia mostly, and when I examine them, I see large blisters on the skin and even in the airways. I've never seen this before. I had seven people admitted just yesterday and I am worried. One of them died last night. I'm not supposed to do autopsies, but I did one anyway on that man. He was 30 and healthy, but when I opened him up, his tissues had melted. Something is being done to them."

Dame Edith struggled to connect the dots. What did the presumed murder of a Saudi runaway princess have to do with young male inmates developing life threatening pulmonary problems? She wondered if her old bones could bear the weight of this knowledge. What should she do?

The doctor continued. "I don't know what to do. I can put in my resignation tomorrow, but I don't want to do that until someone knows what is happening to these poor people, someone who has the power to investigate what is going on. Which is why I am here."

The doctor was reviewing all the points he intended to make, counting them off with his fingers. "Oh, there is one other thing. Each of these men has emitted the smell of strong garlic." He remained seated, his back ramrod straight and inches from the back of the chair but his facial muscles seemed to soften. Was it the effect of relief at being able to tell someone what he had participated in? She noted that he was a younger man than she had guessed at the hearing. How could he bear to be complicit in this craziness?

"Wait right here. There is someone who needs to hear this." Dame Edith rang Donald MacKenzie. "Can you come to my office right now?" The urgency in her voice brought the result she desired.

"I'm on my way." Minutes later Donald knocked on the door and entered. "Are you all right?" The worry on his face moved her.

"Quite all right. But I want you to hear from this man, the physician at the Devon camp who testified before us this week." She turned to the doctor. "This is MP Donald MacKenzie from Glasgow, a chemical engineer in his previous life. Doctor, will you please repeat what you told me about the seven men who were admitted to your clinic in the past week."

As Donald heard the symptoms the doctor described, his face seemed to lose its color. "Mustard," he muttered. "Oh, my God! Human subjects."

"They were never alone with me, always the officer of the camp or one of his assistants was present recording what I said about their condition, photographing the records I kept on them."

Dame Edith was on the phone consulting with the legal expert on her committee. "But can we seize the medical records for the Devon camp? Clare got a court order to suspend the adoptions until the courts can hear our case. We must be able to get a court order to suspend whatever is going on there with the young men…Yes, please. Send a military convoy if necessary."

Dame Edith was processing what they had learned verbally. "If selected young men are being used as human subjects and are being exposed to mustard gas, where in God's name did whoever is doing this acquire the gas? And why would they use it?"

"Porton Downs." That much was clear to Donald. He knew Porton Downs labs were not to conduct research into offensive military weapons. "I suppose one could argue that using existing stocks of mustard gas on human subjects might enable them to assess how best to counter the effect of these weapons?" He was talking to himself. "But mustard is a weapon from World War I. It surely wouldn't be used today." Now he turned to the doctor.

"For how long have men been coming to you with these symptoms?"

"About a week."

"We know it often took days for the symptoms to become full blown during the war, so let's estimate that whatever is going on there has been going on for at least ten days." Donald took out his phone and dialed the intermediary Hugh used to reach Andrew Shale, mumbling to Dame Edith, "I need to make a call, if you'll excuse me?" He moved to the farthest corner of her office and spoke in shorthand: "Mustard gas from Porton Downs tested on human subjects. Call me." Then he paced.

Dame Edith had an idea. MI-5 was one of the most

independent government agencies. She doubted they'd be happy about Saudi security forces operating on their soil. And they would be capable of entering the camp on their own authority under one pretense or another. Hugh's contact there might be a place to start. She opened her door and asked her aide to find Hugh and bring him here immediately. The woman was off like Mercury and back in twenty minutes with Hugh, good old Hugh, who, once the situation had been explained to him, began trying to reach his contact.

The doctor, observing their activity, slowly relaxed against his chair. "I should probably be starting back. I can't participate in what's going on there any longer. I am ready to make a sworn statement, but I'm afraid if I don't return, they will suspect I've been here and begin to cover their activities."

"My good man," Hugh stood in front of him as though ready to restrain him, "they may cover *you*. I think you should be under police protection beginning now."

CHAPTER 51

Hugh's friend at MI-5 absorbed the information the camp doctor had provided but made no comment about what MI-5 might do to retrieve the medical records and/or rescue the men subjected to exposure to chemical weapons. He reminded Hugh that he might be in Parliament, but they were His Majesty's secret service, emphasis on 'secret.' He ended the conversation with, "You're going to have to trust me on this, Hugh." That felt insufficient.

They were a small group of dedicated people but that couldn't be enough to go up against the Saudi government, the Ultra Party, and Britain's foremost chemical weapons laboratory. Surely four MPs, an expert on Britain's treatment of asylum seekers, a random Home Office official, and the doctor at Britain's best known asylum camp were inadequate to the task?

They might win improved conditions at this camp but lose on dozens of other equally important issues—private corporations controlling the detention camps, absence of oversight, children of detainees placed for adoption, foreign governments and the richest people in the world controlling who won power in British elections.

Clare had joined them. She summarized their predicament. "It's like the dikes that hold back the sea, which has been rapidly rising, have been springing multiple leaks, and we don't have enough fingers to plug them all."

Donald, for whom climate change was never more than one thought away from his consciousness, found her metaphor apt. It applied to every island nation, every place with a coastline—about to be inundated and without enough fingers to plug the holes in the seawalls and hold back the flood. They must turn the political tide.

CHAPTER 52

Ibrahim walked during his lunch hours, staying within the area officially marked as "Access Permitted." He glanced casually at the building where the mustard gas canisters were destroyed but saw nothing unusual except for the van with the SS logo and discreet signage that read SmartSecurity. A few days earlier he saw someone on a stretcher hurriedly carried to the back of the van while a line of young Arab men who were coughing climbed into middle of the van.

What was going on here? His instinct made him wary. That night he phoned his former boss and they met at the same pub and walked the same roadway to talk in private.

When he described what he had seen, his friend asked if he had thought whether he was willing to go public and tell people in government what he had observed.

He'd never thought about that. He'd never been an advocate, a dissenter, a person who expressed differences of opinion readily. And since that day in Damascus, his default response when feeling distrustful or in danger was to make detailed plans how to get himself and his family away to some place safe. Flight was always preferable to confrontation. Staying? The word brought up the news video of the two men he had worked beside who had stayed, their bodies sagging from nooses, swinging listlessly with the air. Speaking out? What would happen to him? To his family? Would they be carried to the asylum camps? He focused on doing superior work and pleasing his supervisors. He was not someone to take chances.

His former boss could see Ibrahim's distress at the thought. He re-calculated and tried another approach that might be less threatening. "What if you submitted a sworn statement about what you saw, no speculation? What if your identity was kept secret? If I could guarantee you that Porton Downs wouldn't know who made the report, could you make a statement?"

Ibrahim's voice was raised and angry. "You knew everything about me before I called you about the job. Everything. Even though I had told no one what had happened to me in Damascus. How the hell do you expect me to trust that Porton Downs would not know it was me who made the statement?" He turned and walked rapidly back to his car, turned on the engine but let it idle as he reviewed his options.

The passenger door opened and his former boss slid into the front seat. "If they are doing experiments with chemical weapons on young men—Arabs or any other ethnicity—you are implicated if you shut your eyes to it. You are between a rock and a hard place, my friend. You may lose your job if you speak out, but you will lose your soul if you don't. Think about it. But don't delay. People's lives may be at stake." He left without waiting for Ibrahim to respond.

CHAPTER 53

Mohammed had not seen Amar since the break-in. He had moved from the old neighborhood and not frequented the same football pitch. He rode different Tube lines from Jennifer's house to the restaurant and home. He kept his hair reddish brown and worked at perfecting his English. He and Damir had started cooking at Jennifer's, making the evening meal that all three of them ate together. For some reason it seemed more nourishing that way and the conversation made him more comfortable speaking English.

Each night they watched the news before bed, but the press said nothing about those behind the break-in at the Devon camp. That seemed strange to Mohammed. Men driving seven vans to transport asylum seekers to another country? Other men breaking into a government facility? And no one held responsible?

CHAPTER 54

The doctor returned after a two-day sick leave. Five more young men sat in the waiting room coughing their lungs out. Warily he examined them. Hugh's caution that he himself might be in danger felt like a weight on his chest, but he'd received a message from the MPs asking him to stall his resignation for two weeks, no explanation.

On his second day back in the infirmary he had the distinct feeling that something was different at the Devon camp. You could feel it in the brittleness of the air, like it was charged with electricity and every step you took might shock you. Unfamiliar faces replaced the officers in charge and unfamiliar people accompanied the matrons on their nightly rounds. Rumor had it that Officer Pendleton had been detained.

The women in Barrack #24 sensed a change in their matron. In the days that followed the break-in, discipline in the camp had included body cavity searches. Matrons patted the women down vigorously. They were required to stand in long lines and one by one pull up their burqas and bend over while the matrons' rubber gloved fingers invaded their private parts and probed for secreted things, they were never told what. Some of the matrons were uncomfortable having such intimate contact with their charges. One of them whispered to Ana, "I'm sorry, dearie, but our orders are specific. They think some of you are working with the terrorists."

Terrorists. Who are the terrorists? It was a complicated question and Ana was not clear about the answer. It was offensive to be checked like this, offensive to be held here, prisoners of the longest running democracy in the Western world. But, like every other indignity, she found herself getting accustomed to it. What you can tolerate keeps expanding. You keep going, she observed.

The chill of winter was in the air the day that the matron, going about her usual routine, was accompanied by another woman who wore British street clothes and spoke into a device while she photographed the women and the interior of the barrack. That woman actually helped an older woman who was breathing heavily to settle on her cot and asked her, "Do you need to see the doctor, love?" Such concern was so unusual that two of the inmates, overhearing her, grinned at each other.

A van drove into camp through the service entrance the following evening and unloaded its cargo of young men. It had to be about 5:30 (17:30) and it was already dark. The new woman accompanying the matron asked if anyone had seen this van before. Another woman reminded her that they were usually back in their barrack by 5:10 (17:10). Unlikely they would have seen it through the shutters that were kept nearly closed.

CHAPTER 55

The Gang of Four gathered in Dame Edith's office for a debriefing. Hugh strode back and forth before the other three who were seated, Clare and Dame Edith on the leather sofa and Donald on the leather chair perpendicular to the sofa. Hugh carried a glass of Glenfiddich in his left hand. With his right he gestured like an orchestra conductor, pointing to one and then the other of them.

"My MI-5 contact was, as you predicted (he pointed to Dame Edith) was at the boiling point when I told him of the doctor's testimony that the Saudi Mafia control what happens to Saudi asylum seekers. His people were at the camp today following the camp staff like bloodhounds, sniffing out and documenting what was going on there.

"Clare, getting the injunction on further adoptions was brilliant. So was your strategy of expanding our ranks by recruiting those swinging back and forth to join us in opposition. Those sixteen female MPs you've been meeting with have petitioned to visit the other camps. SmartSecurity and the other private corporations are, it is rumored, considering exiting this business.

"And, Donald, were it not for your Sussex professor's tips about the Saudi Mafia and the gigantic piles of money flowing into the coffers of the Ultra Party from billionaire businessmen (and women) from the autocrats of the Middle East, we'd not have a clue about that big picture.

"Andrew Shale is persona non grata around here since the break-in—some of our peers suggest he was behind the whole operation. Through a third party I have learned that he knows—wait for it—Ana Amara! He and Amnesty International are pushing hard to get her released. She's been conducting her investigative research using the false identity of another asylum seeker. It's a risky strategy, trying to get her released. If they find out who she is, those in power will want to get rid of her. The woman has been investigating for almost a year now. Andrew claims that before she went undercover, she had studied strategies for memorizing details of the stories of people she interviewed. By now she must have a hell of a lot of information stored in that head of hers. We must locate her before they do.

"Which brings me to my anonymous informer who pointed us to Porton Downs. MI-5 was not interested in pulling on that thread—that is the metaphor you proposed we learn to use, is it not, Dame Edith?" When she nodded, he continued. "But the Home Office chap, Aaron Gershon, who testified to your committee after visiting the Devon camp, he might still be able to get back into the camp on the pretense of conducting an audit of the funds expended to maintain the camps. He's champing at the bit to get in there. If we can get him in tomorrow, he'd be able to ride the coattails of MI-5 and gain access to the women's barracks. That is, if we are lucky."

"Is Gershon ready to go that soon?" Donald's stomach had been flipflopping all week with the drama. Living on his stockpile of cheese and biscuits might also have had something to do with it.

"He's ready and waiting for our list of questions he needs to find answers to."

Clare pulled out a notebook and pen. "Call them out and I'll write them down. I always got high marks for penmanship," she said.

"Locate Ana Amara, priority #1."

"Find the fathers, especially those who the doctor has been seeing at his infirmary. What are they doing at Porton Downs?"

"Get the names and countries of origin of people held there."

"Learn who has been pregnant, who's been raped by camp officials, who's been separated from their children."

"Names of the perpetrators."

"Ana Amara's false identity."

Hugh had been recording their responses. With this he turned off his recording device. "There's a lot resting on this man," he said. Then he phoned Aaron Gershon.

CHAPTER 56

Aaron slept only a little and what sleep he had was troubled with nightmares. He made the five-hour drive to Devon in the dark and arrived at the camp at eight a.m. He was armed with spread sheets and recording devices all stuffed in a satchel dangling from a shoulder strap to make him resemble as much as possible a nerdy accountant.

Hugh had pre-arranged with his MI-5 contact that Aaron would have access to the barracks and the people in them, accompanied by an MI-5 officer. It was Sunday, when they did not have to go to their workplaces. He started with the barracks nearest the service entrance that had been the exit for fifty-five women from the camp nearly two months ago. He would enter a barrack, go bed to bed and ask the occupants to write their names, countries of origin, ages, family members in proper spaces on the sheets and then pass the clipboard to the next person. The women's barracks were nearest the service entrance. Andrew Shale had suggested a way he might identify Ana Amara: ask if any of them have two brothers, the eldest named Mohammed and the younger named Damir. Certainly she would respond?

Aaron made it through ten barracks by 1:30 (13:30). No one had responded to the question. It was clear he could not make it through all thirty of the women's barracks, much less the men's, at this pace. The MI-5 official accompanying him suggested they divide up the remaining twenty women's barracks and agreed to ask the question, though he did not see the point of it.

Aaron moved across the field to Barrack #21, working his way through to #30. He was pleased at how many of the women were filling in his sheets, providing their information. At least something useful was coming from this exhausting day.

Nothing unusual occurred until he reached Barrack #24. There his question produced a sharp intake of breath from a woman seated on a cot near where he was standing. For a moment they had eye contact and then she looked away. She seemed to be fumbling underneath her burqa for something. Sure enough, as he moved past her to the next row he felt her tugging his arm. "Sir," she said, "I think you dropped this." She placed a very small electronic box in his hand, then said she had forgotten to sign the sheet. She wrote rapidly. She was from Syria, had no family but a brother Mohammed. She licked her finger and smeared her name just enough to draw attention to it. Then she moved back to her cot and he moved on.

Was this woman Ana? The smudged name bore no resemblance. He pulled out his phone and took a photo of her, stuffing his phone into a pocket before anyone might notice and moved on collecting the information he was there to gather.

Barrack #30 was his last stop. He looked for his MI-5 escort but didn't see him. The armed camp guards in their camouflage were waiting when he exited Barrack #30 and escorted him to his car.

By prearrangement with the MPs he stopped in the first town on his way back to London and, using the burner phone they had provided him, sent photos of page after page of the female residents in Barracks 1-10 and 20-30 to Hugh and to Andrew Shale to be shared with Amnesty. He took a photo of the tiny device the woman in Barrack #24 had given him and sent it with the photo he had taken of her as well. He regretted not having the sheets of information on Barracks 11-19 and wondered where the MI-5 fellow taking that part of their census had disappeared to.

He could barely suppress a smile of satisfaction. Of the six things he was asked to do, he'd accomplished only half, but they were the most important, in his opinion. His right hand felt in his pants pocket for the digital device the woman had passed him. He remembered with chagrin that her fingerprints could be on the device and pulled his hand away. Could it be a camera? If so, the day in Devon had been very profitable.

When Aaron returned from his "sick day" to his office the following morning, his boss was waiting. "You're wanted upstairs," he told him. "Now."

He had known he might pay a high price for yesterday's adventure. Two uniformed police officers stood outside the upstairs office. His mind reviewed what might be on his computer that could hurt others. Too late anyway. As he anticipated, he was informed that his career in government service was over. The officers would escort him from the building with the contents of his desk that were being boxed as they spoke.

When they left him in the parking garage stripped of his government ID with a cardboard box holding little more than framed photos of Marissa and the kids and his favorite coffee mug, the shorter officer murmured, "Have a nice day, sir."

They waited until his car exited the government parking garage. Using the burner phone he called the intermediary he used to contact Andrew Shale to caution him. Then he phoned Marissa. "Think we can live on your salary for a while?" he asked her.

CHAPTER 57

The Gang of Four gathered in Dame Edith's office. Her coffee was superior to Hugh's. For afternoon meetings they went to Hugh's because he served them quality Scotch.

Hugh had been talking on a secure line with his MI-5 contact and laid out for the others what had transpired and the decisions before them. He reported to them Aaron Gershon's firing, the tiny camera passed to Gershon, the photo of the woman Gershon thought was Ana Amara, and her location and the name she was known by at the Devon camp.

"I've been summoned to meet with the Prime Minister at 11. We need to determine what we are asking from him. He may be in a mood to bargain."

"We want an end to family separation. We want Ana released. We want our democracy back—an end to our elections being won by the party bringing in the most money from billionaire autocrats." Clare was on a roll.

Donald MacKenzie interrupted her. "Don't you mean Saudi, Syrian, and Gulf States autocrats?"

Clare retorted, "Are you implying that our homegrown British billionaires who also bought our last election are a higher order of scum?"

"No, but foreigners buying our elections concerns me more." Donald responded. The room was tense. They had kept in check their differences to pursue their common goal of exposing and stopping the Ultra Party's asylum policy, but now the solemn realization that they now must use the modicum of power their persistence had achieved and bargain with the Ultras left them uncertain what to be willing to barter away and what they were bedrock committed to. They were also exhausted after months of focus on asylum seekers at the expense of other issues of more concern to their constituents.

Dame Edith interjected, "I somehow doubt the Prime Minister is going to be negotiating with Hugh over how he finances his party. Perhaps, Hugh, you should focus on the treatment of asylum seekers. You have the camera and the photos someone took with it?"

"No. Gershon passed the camera to MI-5 who are keeping the contents to themselves, other than informing me that they document the doctor's story of young men taken by van and returning coughing and one on a stretcher. We do have Gershon's photo of the woman which he took with his own phone, meaning the Ultras probably can also identify her. His phone was obviously being monitored. He did send me photos of the sheets residents filled out. One of them identifies the woman Gershon believes to be Ana."

"If we can get her out of there and to a safe place, she will be a major resource on the camps. Can Amnesty find that safe place?"

"I don't know. I have been unable to reach Andrew Shale." Dame Edith and Hugh were having a dialog now while Clare and Donald watched them.

"There's always the media."

"Yes, but I must leave for #10 now. I guess we have consensus that Ana's release is priority?" The others nodded their assent.

When Hugh had left, Dame Edith telephoned Jennifer to tell her that they believed Ana had been found. She cautioned Jennifer that this was not public information and assured her that getting her out of the Devon camp and to safety was their priority.

She could hear Jennifer sobbing. "It's going to be all right, love, I promise. I'll be back to you."

When she clicked off, she chided herself for making a promise that was beyond her power to keep.

CHAPTER 58

Ibrahim had begun keeping notes in a small spiral notebook that he kept in his breast pocket. Anyone looking at it would find it gibberish. Each line had letters followed by three sets numbers. Only he could decipher this record: C meant coughing, L meant limping, S meant stretcher-borne. The numbers read from right to left and represented the day, month, time, and number of people that corresponded with the letters. He reasoned that having a daily record of the young men arriving at Porton Downs might be useful if he decided he must share his information.

This morning when he made his daily walk through the grounds and glanced at the building where the mustard gas was being destroyed, there was no van with the SmartSecurity SS logo parked in its usual spot.

CHAPTER 59

When Hugh arrived at #10 Downing Street, he was ushered into the private office of the Prime Minister. He was not the only person the Prime Minister had invited to this meeting. The executive director of the nation's security and intelligence services stood and extended his hand. Hugh found his presence confusing and concerning. He shook hands with both men and then took a seat where the Prime Minister indicated. The Prime Minister wasted no time.

"We are well aware that you dislike our policy toward asylum seekers and are doing your utmost to undermine it. But we need to remind you that we were elected the majority party and our policies have the support of the British public. I have invited you here to make it clear to you that the secret services serve at my direction—isn't that correct?" He sent a penetrating look at the director who nodded in reply. "We are aware that the administrators of one of the detention camps have permitted some irregular activity and we are prepared to curb that activity at that location. The director of SmartSecurity has been so informed."

Hugh broke in. "Exactly what changes are you making at the Devon camp, may I ask? Will children continue to be separated from their parents and adopted without parental permission? Will asylum seekers continue to be used as human guinea pigs for chemical and biological weapons tests at Porton Downs? Will the Saudi government continue to exercise power over Saudi nationals in the camp regardless of the basic rights the British government guarantees to refugees and asylum seekers?" Hugh was trying to keep his voice low and to sound reasonable, but his anger was stronger than he had anticipated and his words flew from his mouth like wasps.

"My dear sir, the separation of children and adopting them out is a popular policy. 'Nits breed lice, you know.'" The Prime Minister turned to the man from the Joint Intelligence Organization, "Wasn't that the expression our American friends used when they needed to get rid of their indigenous population? It's a beautiful irony—we take the children of dissidents and troublemakers and disperse them to Western families where they will grow up happy capitalists—and Christians as well, at least those that get adopted by Americans." He chuckled at his own humor. "And, adding to the pool of adoptable children makes childless couples ecstatic in this time of epidemic levels of infertility among Europeans. It's a win-win policy. As for your concern about 'human guinea pigs,' let me remind you that British citizens were used in tests of LSD and other hallucinogens—and I believe those Porton Downs experiments were conducted within your lifetime. It is Science, my man!"

"Your final issue, about Saudi influence in our camps, is of concern, of course, particularly to the MI-6. They've been wanting to bring down the Saudi government since King Saud, if memory serves me. But I can assure you, the British people will not believe that their government allows any other government to overrule its management of government institutions like the detention centers. They won't believe you no matter what scurrilous, cockamamie story you sell to the liberal media." The Prime Minister strolled the length of the room and then turned and walked up to Hugh, towering over the seated MP.

"I wanted to let you and your socialist rabble-rousers know that the Joint Intelligence Organization has identified those involved in the terrorist act at the Devon Detention Center last month. MI-5 is apprehending all of them as we meet. You may be aware that the mastermind of this operation was the woman you've shown such interest in, Ana Amara. Now, was there something you wanted to ask me?"

The Prime Minister stood in front of Hugh, tall and quite fit for a man in his mid-fifties. Over his shoulder Hugh noticed dozens of sports trophies displayed in his bookcases. Judging by Hugh's inability to respond, he guessed the Prime Minister had won another one. Ana Amara charged with being the mastermind behind the break-in at the Devon camp? In minutes the PM had demolished Hugh's confidence that the Gang of 4 was positioned to win concessions from the Prime Minister. Hugh's face looked grim and he seemed to have aged in the course of this meeting. "So nothing will change in the administration of the camps?"

"SmartSecurity will hire new staff for the Devon facility who will be cautioned to keep their pants zipped or they will be let go. How we handle the long-term residents is a conundrum. The government doesn't want to pay for their maintenance, but what shall we do with them? We've been negotiating with Canada and Ireland who have announced their readiness to accept refugees in large numbers. They hold the peculiar idea that taking in all these asylum seekers will benefit their economy!"

"Can Ana Amara be among those sent to Ireland or Canada?" Hugh was grasping for straws.

"What can you offer to compensate if we don't put on trial the mastermind of a terrorist attack on a facility integral to His Majesty's Government?"

"I must consult my colleagues. Can I get back to you?"

"You will need to let me know in the next hour before we go public with the mass arrests." The Prime Minister turned from Hugh and walked to his desk, sat, and began looking at some papers. It was his signal that the meeting was over. He buzzed for a young aide who escorted Hugh from the building. As he slid into his car, Hugh realized he'd been so shaken he had forgotten his British civility. He'd not shaken hands with the two men.

Back in his office in Westminster as he waited for his colleagues to assemble, he tried to come up with a proposal that would at least salvage Ana from this catastrophic conclusion to their nine-month campaign to help asylum seekers. He could come up with nothing.

Dame Edith, however, had an idea. "Amnesty and Human Rights Watch will surely launch major campaigns on Ana's behalf. What if we offered their silence in exchange for her receiving asylum in Ireland?"

"Would they agree to that?" Donald MacKenzie was dubious.

"Can you call Andrew Shale and find out?"

"I'm afraid he seems to have disappeared. He himself might have been picked up in this MI-5 dragnet. But we could call their London offices. We've only fifteen minutes." Hugh was pacing from the desk to the door and back, moving stiffly, his muscles rigid with anxiety.

"Are we in agreement to try this?" Dame Edith surveyed the room, receiving nods from the other three. Then she had her secretary place two calls. Hugh took one and she herself the other. It took time to explain the situation, but Amnesty and Human Rights Watch both agreed to the plan. Then Hugh called the Prime Minister, who sounded quite happy to hear from him.

They sat in silence, deflated and depressed. Dame Edith turned on the television and muted it until "BREAKING NEWS" crossed the screen.

"The Prime Minister has announced that early this morning MI-5, aided by local police, raided homes in the London area and arrested fifty-some people charged with participating in the terrorist break-in to the detention center near Devon more than a month ago. They will be charged with terrorism and, under our new law, some may receive the death penalty."

An aide rushed into the room. "It's Jennifer on the phone for you, Dame Edith. She says Mohammed was just arrested at her home. She sounds quite frantic. Can you speak with her, ma'am?"

CHAPTER 60

The news cycle the following day included a portion of an interview with Andrew Shale who spoke from Cork, Ireland, where he was living in exile. He denounced the British government's crackdown on refugees and the dragnet operation conducted by MI-5 that had arrested young immigrant men who had conducted a nonviolent raid on a detention camp that was violating international law in its treatment of asylum seekers.

Jennifer watched the broadcast with Damir. Neither of them had slept much the previous night. Damir suggested they take a walk so they could talk freely.

It was one of those damp, wintery days London is known for where the chill penetrates your bones no matter how many layers you are wearing. They both walked briskly.

Dame Edith had called before they left the house to inform Jennifer of the arrangement Hugh had made with the Prime Minister to release Ana to the Irish government in exchange for the human rights groups remaining silent about her case and what she had learned in the camp. As they walked away from the surveillance devices in the house, Jennifer told Damir this new information. They agreed it was at best a Pyrrhic victory. Ana would be spared prosecution as the alleged mastermind of an act of terrorism, but she would be confined to Ireland, separated from Damir and Jennifer, and Mohammed would be prosecuted and likely found guilty. Perhaps he would be sentenced to the death penalty.

The online media was full of gruesome stories about the "terrorists" who conducted the raid, claiming that they were linked to the worst of the many guerrilla groups that had formed since 2003 to use massive violence against civilians gathered in ordinary public places. A mug shot of Mohammed had gone viral. The accompanying story linked him with his sister although her name, oddly, was not supplied. The story claimed that they were co-initiators of the break-in at the Devon camp.

Things were moving very fast and Mohammed and Ana were in grave danger.

"The best news is that Ana is alive. We could move to Ireland," Jennifer proposed tentatively.

"But Mohammed will need our presence here in London. We must find the money to pay for an outstanding barrister to argue his case."

Damir's earnestness and naivete moved Jennifer, and she looked over at his face feeling almost maternal. How young he is, she thought. Yet he has gone through so much—the war, his mother's death, his father's execution, Ana's disappearance, and now at least one and perhaps both of his siblings imprisoned and to be tried for treason. It is so unfair for this young man not yet out of high school to have to bear so much trauma and suffering. I am all he has now, she thought.

Their conversation meandered as they tried to problem-solve what to do to help Mohammed. Dame Edith had offered to secure a lawyer friend of hers whose specialty was immigration law. He probably would be able to identify other barristers who argued terrorism cases. She was certain they could put together a defense fund. Mohammed's case might be just the vehicle for exposing how asylum seekers were treated under the Ultra Party.

Bless her, the woman just wouldn't give up. Jennifer found herself weeping. She wept for their situation, of course, but also for these good people who had come into her life—Damir and

Mohammed and Dame Edith and her Three Musketeers in the House of Commons. My love for Ana has carried me into such unfamiliar territory and taught me to feel responsibility for strangers. It has expanded my heart. Whatever happens now, I am bound to them, to all the Amaras and the other unnamed asylum seekers. There was something soothing in that realization, although she couldn't find words to explain why.

They turned the corner and walked back to the house, walking against the wind.

The next morning she awakened before her alarm. Her phone was blinking with messages. Tentatively she returned the most recent one.

"This is Kathryn Goyle with *The Guardian*. I wonder if you'd care to comment about the statement released by Ana Amara this morning."

"I know nothing about any statement from Ana."

"I will read it to you: 'I, Ana Amara, am a journalist. My research has focused in recent years on the plight of refugees and asylum seekers from Muslim majority countries coming to the UK. I am charged with masterminding a break-in to the asylum camp near Devon where I was held for ten months. To silence me and others who know what is going on in this and other such camps, the Prime Minister has offered to let me take asylum in Ireland. I am rejecting his offer. Truth is what good journalists seek to uncover, no matter the personal cost. I will remain in Britain and face trial and these bogus charges of terrorism. I choose to go to trial to get out to the public the travesties being inflicted on innocent refugees in this nation, the world's oldest democracy.'"

Jennifer, stunned, could only get out, "That's my Ana."

The next message on her phone was from Ireland from the man they'd seen on the telly, Andrew Shale. He spoke rapidly and without pause. "Ana asked me to notify you that Mohammed is here in Cork. He's being granted asylum by Ireland, and the Prime Minister won't seek his extradition. Ana insisted on Mohammed taking her place. She plans to put up a good fight in the courts. I'm not certain what her visitor situation will be but look into it. She should be arriving at Downview Women's Prison in Surrey this afternoon. While you're at it, take a look at the news. I must go. The best to you."

Jennifer knocked vigorously on Damir's door to get him up and, when he appeared sleepy-eyed and wary, she told him the news. Together they went into the sitting room where they could watch the BBC News. The lead story was from Saudi Arabia where the Crown Prince had just been assassinated. The reporter on the ground in Riyadh said rumor had it that the security forces had turned on the royal family.

EPILOGUE

Several months later Ibrahim and his wife Amra talked over breakfast about the stories breaking daily about the detention camps and the forthcoming trials of the young men and the journalist Ana Amara charged with terrorism. The latest news story was that the camp inmates were used as human guinea pigs for experiments with chemical and biological agents at Porton Downs' research labs. The government supported this policy of forcing asylum seekers to be human subjects. They argued that the asylum seekers "volunteering" allowed scientists at Porton Downs to find antidotes to these weapons that would protect the British people if chemical and biological weapons were ever used against Britain.

Ibrahim fingered the notebook he'd been keeping with the numbers of men brought to the lab in SmartSecurity vans each day and their condition. "Should I come forward and provide this evidence in the trial of these so-called terrorists?" he asked Amra. It would probably mean he would lose his job, perhaps be unemployable. Whistleblowing had serious consequences.

Amra, who had found a job teaching Arabic at a local community college, needed to leave for work. She pulled on her raincoat, kissed the top of his head, picked up her keys, and turned to him as she stood in the doorway. she said. "See you tonight." Then she smiled and closed the door behind her.

NOTES

Readers may be interested in the following resources on this subject, presented here to link the fictional story with a few related published sources.

https://www.gov.uk/government/news/new-asylum-accommodation-contracts-awarded.

BBC Four documentary on Youtube "Inside Porton Downs, Britain's Secret Weapons Research Facility" by Michael Moseley (2016).

July 20, 2019 http://www.arabnews.com/node/958591/economy. See also the New Arab, April 29, 2015 https://www.alaraby.co.uk/english/news/2015/5/1/who-are-the-richest-arabs-in-the-uk. Also, of interest is this article on the billion dollar Saudi empire in US which is secret https://www.independent.co.uk/news/business/news/revealed-saudi-royals-secret-1bn-us-empire-7817936.html.

On the 2019 UK asylum requirement of having money, see https://www.gov.uk/government/news/changes-to-the-immigration-rules--3.

In February 2015 the Home Secretary asked Stephen Shaw to conduct a review of the welfare of vulnerable individuals in detention. The Minister of State for Immigration James Brokenshire reported the results here: https://www.parliament.uk/written-questions-answers-statements/written-statement/Commons/2016-01-14/HCWS470. On Stephen Shaw's follow up 2018 report, https://www.libertyhumanrights.org.uk/news/press-releases-and-statements/liberty%E2%80%99s-analysis-today%E2%80%99s-shaw-review-immigration-detention-%E2%80%9Cwe.

"Assad" by George Parker in the New Yorker, April 15, 2018 –For Human Rights Watch data on cw, https://www.nytimes.com/2019/05/11/world/middleeast/syria-torture-prisons.html--torture and secret executions.

https://science.howstuffworks.com/mustard-gas2.htm.

Stephen Dorrill, *MI6: Inside the Covert World of Her Majesty's Secret Intelligence Service* (New York: Simon & Schuster, 2000, 520 and 615.

ABOUT THE AUTHOR

G. C. Eick worked on foreign and military policy on Capitol Hill in Washington, DC for ten years before earning a Ph.D. from the University of Kansas and becoming a Professor of History. Her international travel included teaching from 2017-2020 at Dzemal Bijedic University in Mostar, Bosnia and Herzegovina, and she teaches in Wichita State Wichita State University's Life Long Learning Program. Her books include the prize-winning *Dissent in Wichita: The Civil Rights Movement in the Midwest, 1954-72* (University of Illinois Press, 2001/2008), *They Met at Wounded Knee: The Eastmans' Story* (University of Nevada Press, 2020), winner of the Donald and Bertha Coffin Award. She also writes fiction, both historical and speculative thrillers. Eick's novels are *Maybe Crossing:* (Blue Cedar Press, 2015), *Finding Duncan* (Blue Cedar Press, 2015), *The Set Up: 1984, Britain's Biggest Drug Bust, Classified Until 2064* (Blue Cedar Press, 2018), *Dark Crossings* (Blue Cedar Press, 2022), and the forthcoming *Cora's Crossing*, expected in 2024.

She lives in Wichita, Kansas with her husband, poet Michael Poage.